THE BOY WHO BOUGHT IT

AN ESTELA NOGALES MYSTERY

CHERIE O'BOYLE

And in *The Boy Who Bought It*, University psychologist, Estela Nogales is all set for a relaxing summer break, maybe join a gym, adopt a new hobby, or curl up with a few good books. The fun she anticipates does not include identifying the dead body her dogs discover washed up on the beach. And she certainly has no reason to expect the mystery will lead her right back to the quiet neighborhood of Arroyo Loco and her friends there. The boy who bought it may have gotten what was coming to him, and at the hands of those he wronged, but as the investigation unravels the clues there turns out to be more to the story.

Other books in the Estela Nogales mystery series

> *Fire at Will's* (2014)
> *Iced Tee* (2015)
> *Missing Mom* (2016)
> *Deadly Disguise* (2017)

... and a prequel short story: *Back for Seconds?*

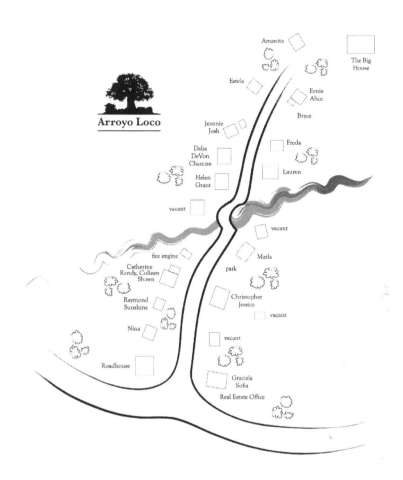

Arroyo Loco

Amanita

The Big House

Estela

Ernie
Alice

Bryce

Jeannie
Josh

Freda

Delia
DeVon
Chamise

Lauren

Helen
Grant

vacant

vacant

Marla

fire engine

park

Catherine
Randy, Colleen
Shawn

Raymond
Sunshine

Christopher
Jessica

vacant

Nina

vacant

Roadhouse

Graciela
Sofia

Real Estate Office

PROLOGUE

An unhurried push, and the bundle wrapped in a ragged sheet and tied with blue dock line rolled off the gunwale. Fog and a gentle sea quieted any splash when the weight slipped beneath the gray-green surface. The mournful cry of one seagull serenaded the body as it disappeared into the depths. No loving words of farewell were spoken, no remembrances uttered. Wavelets lapped at the bow as the boat turned, now heading toward shore.

CHAPTER ONE

Careful not to snag my favorite shirt on the rusting wire of the cyclone fence, I stepped through the opening cut there long ago. My two leashed border collies leapt after me, excited to begin their run on the unofficial and somewhat scuzzy dog beach. Brilliant in the mid-morning sun, Morro Rock shimmered above us. Peregrine falcons circled its outcroppings, carrying food to their half-grown nestlings. A few of those teetered on rock ledges, eyeing their parents, and stretching recently feathered wings.

I unleashed Shiner and Scout at the same moment that an athletic woman with a pony-tail jogged past us and waved. Her Dalmatian, Daisy, trotted along behind. As is usual at any dog beach or park, we humans are more likely to know the dogs' names than each other's. Comes from hours of standing around chatting, primarily about our dogs while watching them play. Ponytail kept going while I pulled my lucky Giants baseball cap decorated with the 9mm bullet hole over my unruly curls and strolled in the same direction.

Being herding dogs, Shiner and Scout raced ahead, circled Ponytail and came back to me. That's called the "get around" in herding. When circled by a herding dog, your average sheep will double-back to rejoin the flock. Ponytail and Daisy continued on at a steady pace though, so Shiner and Scout gave up the maneuver and returned to me.

It was a perfect day to take my rambunctious dogs on their run. Earlier this morning the usual June gloom of fog had cut visibility to near zero here along the central California coast, but by the time we got to the beach at around eleven, I could see almost all the way to the pier at Cayucos.

Heading toward us at a flying gallop, Shiner's best buddy, Jax, a golden retriever, appeared far up the beach. Although still out of sight, I knew somewhere between us and the pier, Jax's human, Evan, also made his way our direction.

Shiner ran out to meet Jax, both dogs throwing sandy wet front legs over one another's shoulders in gleeful greeting. All three dogs took off running, making giant looping circles, leaping over the latest logs, driftwood, and bits of plastic washed ashore with the tide before dawn. Shiner hit a patch of seaweed in the shallows at the water's edge, splattered through it, slipped, and came up with green smeared across the white ruff at his neck. I ducked too late, and his shake peppered my face with salt water, sand, and dead seaweed. Probably some happy-dog spit mixed in there, too.

Using a relatively clean sleeve to wipe off the plastic lid on my takeout coffee, I took another sip. As long as my dogs were having a good time, I would endure any amount of splattering with gunk. We navigated around a streamlet where the creek coming down from the Coast Range disappeared into the sand on its way to the waves, and the pile of detritus dumped there by the tide. I waved as Evan came into view, still more than fifty yards away. Jax raced around me and headed back to check in with Evan, my dogs in hot pursuit. They circled him and ran toward me again.

I stopped, took a long sip, and gazed out over the ocean, still gray-green from the remnants of fog lingering over the horizon. This was the first day of what I hoped would be a long, relaxing summer break from my stress-filled job as a psychotherapist on a busy university campus. I planned to go for many long walks on the beach, maybe join a gym and get in shape, find an art class or take up a new hobby, and catch up on reading lots of good fiction.

About then it dawned on me that, although the dogs were headed back this way, they had not yet arrived. When I turned to check, both of mine stood just up the beach, their snouts lifted. Smelling something unusual, apparently. Being human, and thus possessing woefully lesser sensory abilities, I blithely ambled north along the beach, smelling nothing but salty sea air.

The tide this morning had been high, and left a lot of debris on shore. A collection of garbage and dead fish had been deposited on the beach. For once, I was grateful for my lesser ability to smell. The dogs were captivated, and I hoped no one was going to roll in anything.

As Evan and I drew closer, I waved again, looking forward to good conversation about dog behavior, or philosophy, or one of our other favorite topics. He pointed behind me, and I looked back. Scout stood, still frozen in place. Shiner, on the other hand, tiptoed gingerly, lifting his paws high, walking toward the odiferous pile of water-logged branches and kelp. Their behavior triggered my suspicion. I may not have their powerful sense of smell, but I am gifted in the interpretation of dog behavior.

The thing is, I know from experience that, like most dogs, Shiner is attracted to the smell of dead things. Scout, on the other hand, hates the whole idea of dead things. Even things

Scout has recently dispatched trigger his disgust. And at that moment, everything in Scout's body language said, "Eew!"

I turned my attention back to Shiner. He finds the smell of dead things appealing, inviting, even compelling. He seeks such things out, especially on the beach, and throws himself upon them, rolling and collecting the smell all over his fur. Then the rest of us are forced to ride home in the same stinky car. Once home, I have to spend an hour scrubbing the disgusting smell off him that he went to such lengths to acquire.

At that moment, Shiner had his head to the ground creeping toward a large log, seeking the object of his attraction.

"Shiner, here!"

He looked at me, and went back to sniffing. My normally obedient dog could not overcome his compulsion to go after dead things. He looked up at me again, guilt written all over his face. Curious. Whatever he'd found could not be just another dead fish.

I walked closer, moving to the side of the pile, trying to see what he'd found. I caught a glimpse of something gray and roundish, fairly large, tucked behind the wet log. A couple of years ago we'd encountered a dead seal on this beach. From what I could see, this object easily matched the size of a seal. Only this didn't exactly look like a seal. Whatever it had once been, it was now entangled in a length of blue nylon dock line.

A ripple of dread ran down my back, and I pulled my cap tighter. I waited for Evan to come up beside me before I looked again.

"What's up, Estela?" he said, as he ambled up in flip flops and clamdiggers. Or maybe those were cargo shorts. With guys, one never knows. He shifted his eyes to follow my gaze.

"What do you think that thing is?" I pointed. By that time, Jax had caught the scent too, and was creeping up behind Shiner. The fur on Jax's shoulders lifted, signaling alarm.

"Something wrapped in a sheet?" Evan suggested.

I tried harder to focus. Maybe my doctor was right, and the time had come to think about that cataract surgery. I walked a few feet closer and saw what Evan meant. A dirty sheet wrapped tightly around the object and tied with dock line. Who would wrap a dead seal like a mummy? And why?

"Jax! Come here Jax!" Evan wasn't having any better luck than I at getting his dog's attention.

My dogs have the "here" command, which they respond to reliably in almost every circumstance. My personal theory is that, to them, "here" means, amble on back, unless you're busy with something else. Luckily, both my dogs and I are semi-bilingual, and we have another word, *"aqui,"* which is for use in emergencies. I like to think that, to the dogs, *"aqui"* means turn around immediately and go directly to that lady who dispenses treats, no matter what, because she sees a danger we don't know about. It's probably more likely they think *"aqui"* means Wowzaa! she has a big handful of treats for us this time! Whatever works.

"Aqui!" I called as though I really meant it this time. Scout finally turned and trotted toward me. Shiner waited until he saw me reach into the small pack in which I carry the treats, and then he raced over, never one to be late when the goodies are handed out. Jax took another sniff at the object, watched his friends, and, mercifully, followed them to us. The dogs received multiple treats and leashes clipped to their collars for their obedient response.

Evan and I gazed at the bundle again. About five feet long, cylindrical, wet, the sheet folded away in one place.

"Looks too big to be a seal," Evan said,

"Why would it be a seal?"

"What's the alternative?"

I let that one percolate for a bit. "Good point."

We stared.

"Too small to be a grown man," I said. "Maybe a woman?"

"Or a child."

"Yikes, I hope not."

"Could be somebody just wanted to get rid of an old carpet. They rolled the carpet up in a sheet and dumped it overboard."

"Yes, that could be. See where that corner is folded over? Coming loose?"

"Sure." Evan tipped his head and twisted his lips, gazing at the loosened sheet.

"Why don't you go over there and pull it back a little more, just enough to see what's in there. Here, I'll hold Jax." I reached for the leash before I noticed Evan's raised eyebrow.

"I'm not going any closer. You go over and see what that thing is," he said.

We were at an impasse. "I thought guys were supposed to do all the scary stuff," I said, mostly kidding.

"You got the wrong guy. We should call someone."

"Yes, but who?"

"Nine-one-one?"

"What if it turns out to be a roll of old carpet?"

Something on the bundle moved. Evan and I both jumped. The loose corner flipped back, flapping in the gentle breeze.

"Listen," I said, "we know from the dogs' behavior that it's almost certainly some kind of dead thing. And look." I pointed skyward where two turkey vultures cruised in on a thermal, tipping their wings, and positioning themselves in lazy circles over the pile of debris. Fifty feet across the beach, three seagulls hopped toward the pile, alternately eyeing our little group and the vultures overhead.

"Agreed," Evan said. "Should we call animal control?"

"You mean because you think it's a seal?"

"Well, I don't want to overreact here. You want to call homicide?"

"Let's call nine-one-one and let them decide whether to call animal control or homicide. Or garbage collection."

"They're going to ask you the nature of your emergency. What are you going to say?'

I'd already pulled out my phone. We couldn't just walk away and leave that thing. "I'm going to say we found a dead body. The way the dogs acted? That thing is no old carpet."

Evan, the dogs, and I were kind of stuck waiting until the deputy sheriff responded. After about fifteen minutes, a white SUV approached on the highway, drove north, u-turned and drove south, then finally selected one of the not-entirely legal parking spaces near the hole cut through the rusty fencing. We waved, but even after the two deputies started our way it took them a good ten minutes to slog through the sand to our position.

They gazed dubiously at our find. They did not have the same faith that Evan and I had in the evidence provided by the dogs and the vultures, so they were not as convinced the bundle contained a dead body. Reluctant to share our conclusion, they moved closer, and one guy closed his hand over his nose. I guess from that close, even humans caught the stench. The other guy focused his phone and took several photographs. Only after that did one reach down and pull back the sheet.

Needless to say, my dogs and I had by then turned our backs and begun walking quickly away, trailed closely by Evan and Jax. We'd done our civic duty by making the phone call and pointing out the location of the bundle. I didn't need the sight of a water-logged body seared into my memory. Especially if it turned out to be a hapless victim of animal cruelty.

"Hey!" came the cry from behind us. Evan turned. I would let him handle it.

"What?"

"Don't go away! We need to ask you some questions!"

"Fine! Okay! We'll wait right here." We stopped, our backs still turned.

Evan and I exchanged a long look. I lifted Shiner's Chuckit from my back pack and loaded it with a ball. As long as I threw the ball in front, the dogs would stay away from the activity behind us.

We played in silence for a few minutes, Evan turning to see what the deputies were doing every once in a while.

"Oh, geez," he muttered.

"What?"

"They're marking off a section of beach all the way down to the water, you know, using that yellow plastic tape?"

"Crime scene tape."

"Yes, that. Here comes one of them. Good morning," he said as a deputy came up on our left. "Why are you marking off so much of the beach?"

"Ahem," the deputy cleared his throat. "Looks like the body must've washed up with the tide early this morning. We're preserving the pathway it might've traveled. Could've washed up there anywhere across that stretch."

I turned slightly, carefully keeping my eyes averted from the location of what the deputy had just referred to as a body. The second deputy was unspooling yellow tape across a stretch of beach about as wide as a four lane highway and from the pile all the way down to the water.

"Now we gotta wait for homicide."

"Homicide," I said. "So it is a human?"

The deputy gave me a puzzled scowl, one eyebrow arched high. What'd you think?"

I could only bow my head. Nothing good about this situation. Shiner chose that moment to shake himself all over, finishing with a flip of his tail that sent wet sand in a stripe across the deputy's uniform.

Evan glanced back over his shoulder at the body. "How do you know it was a homicide?" he asked.

"Huh," the deputy replied. "'S not like somebody can wrap themselves in a sheet like that before jumping into the ocean to drown."

Evan nodded absently and I caught his gaze. "He drowned?" I asked.

"Of course we won't know 'til the medical examiner gets a look. Right now, all we know is he's soaking wet, and very dead. Been that way for a few days, from the smell of it."

I'd had about enough at that point. "Can we go now?" The deputy explained that he'd be more comfortable if we would stay until the detective and the evidence recovery team could get to the scene. The way I figured, it wasn't my job to make sure the deputy felt comfortable. I told him I was a consultant with the sheriff's department, and Evan pointed to where he lived, at the south end of Cayucos, overlooking the beach. We each gave the deputy our phone numbers and told him he could find us either at Evan's house or by phone. We gathered up our leashes and prepared to wander away.

"Hang on a sec." The deputy fished out his phone and snapped a few shots of my sneakers, both top and underside.

"You walked across the path the body likely traveled, so we need these for comparison and elimination purposes." He asked if he could have samples of fur from the two dogs who had approached the victim. Both Jax and Shiner were happy to donate already loose tufts of potential evidence. There was plenty more where that came from. Evan handed the deputy an unused poop bag in which to stash the fur samples.

I looked around trying to see how my dogs and I could get back to our car. Our choices were to wait until the tide went way out, beyond the yellow tape, or try to find an alternative hole in the rusty fence big enough to climb through and then walk along the shoulder of the busy highway.

"Looks like you're stuck," Evan said. "Want to walk up to my place? I can give you a lift to your car."

Not having much choice, I nodded and we set off. Evan and I met on the beach with the dogs a couple of years ago, and known each other only in that setting. Even though his house was nearby, I'd never been there. And since most of what we talked about had to do with the feeding, care, and training of puppies, dog personalities, and dog behavior, we knew almost nothing about each other. As we walked, we let the dogs run ahead, keeping a close eye on their travels. Who knows but there might be another one of those bundles washed up?

CHAPTER TWO

Evan's place turned out to be a somewhat dilapidated bungalow overlooking the beach in south Cayucos. A large deck spanned the width of the house and provided an expansive view of the beach and the ocean beyond. He has often mentioned that his house needs to be painted, and indeed, it would be hard to know where to start. I could see spots that had, at one time, known a coat of paint, but most of the wood had reverted to a naturally-weathered shade of gray. Also, a carpenter would need to be engaged to repair or replace several elements of trim, siding, and even framing, that had come loose or been lost altogether. Far be it from me to judge, as my own house is also in need of steady maintenance. At least the steps to my porch could be navigated in relative safety. Evan's required concentrated attention, stepping only on the far side where the rotting planks still enjoyed some structural integrity.

Once on the deck, I could hardly see through the salt deposits clouding the plate-glass window. Through the clearer center, I could make out a neatly kept interior. Several high-end specialty pans hung over a kitchen bar, too. Hmm, a man who cooks. Interesting.

Deciding against taking three wet sandy dogs inside, I settled on one of the two wobbly Adirondack chairs positioned to maximize views both north and south along the beach. The dogs plopped down beside me on the warm wood of the deck. After a few minutes, Evan set two cups of steaming tea on the table between the chairs.

"Honey lavender," he said.

"I beg your pardon?" But he had already disappeared inside. The tea must be an infusion of honey and lavender, I decided. He returned a moment later and handed me a large pair of binoculars.

"Uh, thanks. Are you going to give me a lesson in identifying birds?"

"Just thought you might like to see what's going on down the beach."

"Ugh! I think I've seen enough for one morning!" I set the binoculars on the table and took up my tea. Didn't want to admit I wasn't even sure which end of the binoculars to look through. I shifted my shoulders away from the probably grisly scene to the south.

We sat in silence for a time, watching the sun finish burning through the last vestiges of coastal fog. Evan kept glancing behind me, keeping an eye on law enforcement's activity. He picked up the binoculars, leaned over, and gave the beach a long look. I made a careful note about which end of the binoculars he was looking through.

"What's happening now?" I asked without turning.

"There's a photographer taking a lot of pictures. One of the deputies is putting things here and there. Little orange cones? I think she's marking various spots."

"She? That's at least a quarter mile away, and you can see she's a she? What are those binoculars, magic?"

17

"Now a couple of guys in white are slogging through the sand. Wonder if they'll be able to get an ambulance or some kind of vehicle out there to pick up the ... the bundle. I think I see a van a long ways farther down."

I turned briefly, no longer able to resist. A fuzzy but familiar broad-shouldered figure trudged toward the pile of debris, staying on the damp and harder sand near the water's edge. "Here, let me see those things." I reached and Evan handed me the binoculars. I put them to my eyes, but could not see a thing.

"You'll need to focus those for your eyes. They're set up to work for me with my glasses."

I had no idea what he was talking about, and turned to him with a scowl.

"Let me show you." He came around behind my shoulders while I put the binoculars back to my eyes. He leaned over, his neatly-trimmed beard scratchy on my cheek. I willed myself not to reach up and rub where it tickled. The guy was just trying to help. "Now, close your right eye, look with your left eye, and turn this focus knob, here, until you can see clearly." He tapped the knob and I put the glasses down to see where he tapped, then put them back up.

"Close my right eye, open my left eye and turn this knob? Shall I pat my head and rub my tummy, too? Are you kidding me?"

He laughed. "No really, close your right eye, and look with your left."

"Okay, fine. I still see nothing. Whoops, there went a flash of something."

"Good, good. Keep trying until you can see with the one eye."

Moving slowly, I finally managed to make the light come back and stay. "All I see is fog."

"There's no fog out there. Here, turn this knob very slowly until something comes into focus."

I moved the knob ever so slightly and suddenly the familiar figure at the other end of the beach jumped into clear view. It was my old friend, Detective Antonio Muñoz, dressed as nattily as usual in a light gray sports jacket, possibly tweed, but hard to say from this distance, even with the binoculars. He picked his way through the driftwood, the front of his sports jacket flying open the like wings on a duck. Those binoculars were so powerful, I swear I could see the pattern on his tie. Before he leaned over the bundle, he took a moment to tuck the tie inside the buttons on his shirt. I wondered how many times a homicide detective has to dip the end of his tie into ghastly remains before he learns to tuck it out of the way.

I took the binoculars from my face and waved. Of course Muñoz had no idea I was there, not to mention he also did not have the benefit of magic binoculars. He made no response.

I put the glasses back to my eyes, entranced with how clearly I could see the tiniest details so far away. The creek where it sank into the sand, the rough bark on a water-soaked log, a guy in a white coat unwrapping the sheet on ... oops. Fortunately, my reactions were quick enough, and I don't think I actually saw any body parts. Maybe some hair. I handed the binoculars off to Evan and extracted my phone from my back pocket.

Muñoz answered on the first ring. I explained the situation, and waved again. He still didn't see me, but he did say I could go on home, and he would stop by later if he had any questions.

"Okay, ready to head home," I said as Evan collected empty cups. "Say, why do you have these binoculars so handy here?" I winked. "Use them to look at bathing beauties on the beach?"

He gave me an irked frown. "Birds, Estela. I use them to look at the shorebirds."

"Isn't that what I just said?"

"Down the side steps," he pointed. "I'll meet you at the car in front."

Well, phooey. I was hoping for a tour inside the bungalow, or at least a quick walk-through.

Finding a dead body was not exactly the carefree start to summer I'd been planning, but now that whole situation was Muñoz's problem. I settled into a comfortable wicker chair on my screened porch with a nice bowl of pasta salad for lunch, my much-anticipated novel, and my beloved dogs curled at my feet. Quickly, I polished off the salad and opened the book.

An hour or so later, I was awakened by the nearby twittering of an unseen bird in the blue oak that grows over my house. Actually, there were several twitterings, a flock of tiny birds. Or so I guessed, not being able to get a good look at any of them. At the ends of the branches, leaves shook, and bits broke off and fell, but I still couldn't see the birds, even when I leaned my head out the door. Maybe, I thought, Evan was onto something. Maybe I should take up birding. Or at least I could go dig Papa's binoculars out of that box on the closet shelf.

The box contained a variety of items, each threatening to distract me from my mission, until at the very bottom I found the dusty binoculars. With a little window cleaner and a good scrubbing with the microfiber I use on my reading glasses, the binoculars were as good as new. I carried them to the porch and peered into the tree. That's when I learned the first lesson

20

in birding. Birds don't usually linger so as to provide the would-be birder with ample opportunity to examine them in detail. They were all gone, off to find food elsewhere.

Since I'd already gone to the trouble to locate the binoculars, and clean them, I kept them to my eyes, fiddling with the focus knob. I found I could focus up close, getting a good look at the dead bugs on the windshield of my rental car. Lifting them to peer down the canyon road, still messing with the focus, I checked out the roofing shingles on Freda Von Leising's cottage, some two hundred feet away. The detail was amazing. Across the road, I could even see a weathered red ball caught in the gutter at Delia's house. Her kids must have lost that a long time ago.

My house sits about a quarter mile up Arroyo Loco Road from the highway that winds through the California coastal mountains between Morro Bay and Atascadero. Nineteen houses line our road, from Graciela's home and real estate office down at the highway to the new McMansion at the very top of the road. I can only see parts of the settlement of Arroyo Loco from my house, and most of the time, that is fully as much as I care to see of the goings-on at my neighbors' homes. I hear enough detail about other people's lives in my counseling practice and prefer to maintain my privacy when at home.

I leaned into my chair and went back to inspecting the detail on Freda's house, one of the few on that downhill side that I could comfortably see from my porch. Although it was only mid-afternoon, the shadows were growing deep in Arroyo Loco canyon, and a light going on in Freda's open bathroom window drew my attention. Her head appeared in the window, swathed in a white bath towel. The precision with which the binoculars brought every aspect into clear view was truly astonishing. I watched, entranced, as Freda unwrapped the towel and bent until her head was out of sight below the level of the sill. I've never been in Freda's bathroom, but it was easy to imagine she was bending over a basin there. She stood again, holding an object and applying it to her head.

Well, would you look at that! All these years Freda has insisted her orange hair was the natural color, even though, and especially at her advanced age, everyone could see the impossibility of that. And here she was, plain as day, applying color to the roots.

Almost as though she felt me looking, Freda turned and slammed the window closed. Yikes! Was it possible she'd seen me? I'd have to stop focusing on people, I decided, and stick to birds. Still captivated with my new toy, I stepped out to my driveway and turned to look at the hills behind our houses. Maybe there would be birds out there in the oaks, or other wildlife wandering the semi-hidden trail system that meandered the length of the canyon. I stood still and focused, slowly panning the oak-covered hills.

CHAPTER THREE

As I peered at the hillside with the binoculars, a flash of blue appeared in the round visual field. I stopped, scanned backwards ever so slightly, and caught it again. Not a bird, but it did move. I took the glasses away and tried to find the object with unaided eyesight. A figure coming down the hill on a spur of the trail. A figure in a blue dress, her blonde bob appearing and disappearing as she crossed behind bushes. It was my neighbor, Helen Auroch. I focused the binoculars on her again. The dress had big blue flowers on it, and Helen was carrying a shovel over one shoulder, a red plastic bucket in the other hand. I sighed, fearing I knew what she'd been up to, out of the sight of her neighbors.

Helen keeps cats. Numerous cats. She claims they all live inside her house, and in the large wire catio connected to the back. Although no one has ever proposed an actual homeowners' association rule about it, we do frown on outdoor cats here in Arroyo Loco. Not only do domestic cats allowed to roam outdoors kill millions of songbirds annually, but the cats themselves too often fall victim to horrific deaths, torn apart alive by hawks and owls, hunted and killed by packs of coyote, infected by disease-carrying ticks or colonized by a whole variety of parasites. In Arroyo Loco, our opinion is, if you care enough to have a cat, you care too much to want them to suffer like that.

In spite of Helen's efforts to keep her cats indoors, she does regularly find tiny dead songbirds in her yard. She knows, as do we all, that very little of the activity in and around our yards goes unobserved by at least one or more neighbors. So I felt certain Helen had found yet another victim of her murderous cats, and climbed the trail behind her house to bury the poor thing in relative privacy. Little did she know I had acquired a new hobby, and the means to spy on her, even from this distance. I'd have to remember to make a snide remark next time I saw her.

My new found hobby opened up all sorts of possibilities. I remembered scenes from that Hitchcock thriller, Rear Window, and how James Stewart had used binoculars to spy on the neighbors in his apartment complex. His spying ultimately led to a conviction that he had seen evidence of a murder, and attempts to cover it up. Great movie.

Then I remembered how the movie ends. Decided maybe I should find a different new hobby. I returned to my screened porch and the novel awaiting me there. I should definitely sit down and read that. First, though, I would go into the yard and play ball with the dogs. After all, their usual morning game had been interrupted.

After a good twenty minutes romping we were all short of breath. Back in the screened porch, I'd gotten a sentence or two into my novel when the gravel in my driveway crunched, alerting me to the arrival of a shop-worn dark sedan. Detective Muñoz arriving. I could only suppose he had come to ask questions about my sad find this morning on the beach. He ambled to the porch and, with one foot, tested the first step with a shiny black loafer. He'd learned the hard way those steps were not always in the finest state of repair.

I invited him to sit, and offered a cold drink, which he declined. Good thing, too, as I so rarely had anything anyone wanted. I think I was down to three cans of off-brand ginger ale and a tiny V8 juice.

The pattern on his tie was tiny Monarch butterflies, by the way, just in case anyone was still wondering. He asked me to outline the scene this morning, which I did, briefly. There really wasn't much to tell.

"Who was it, do you know, yet?" I asked.

He shook his head. "We don't have any missing persons reports in this county matching his description. It does look as though he washed in with the tide, so he could have come from anywhere."

"It was a guy?"

"Oh, yeah, sorry. So you really didn't see him at all?"

"No, sir. He was all wrapped up, and we walked away from there as fast as we could the minute your deputy let us go."

"You and ..." Muñoz pulled his phone from an interior pocket and scrolled. "You and Evan Flamson?"

"Yes, Evan and his dog Jax, plus my two guys. We had quite a crowd out there this morning. We all saw the bundle. And you have no idea who it is, or was?"

Still scrolling, Muñoz only shook his head without looking up.

"That blue rope the bundle was tied with, isn't that the kind of rope used on boats? Like, marine rope? He must have been dumped off a boat, don't you think?"

"That's a good guess, but doesn't narrow down the boy's identity."

"Boy! He was only a boy?"

"Uh, sorry again. Yeah, late teen-age. Possibly as old as twenties. We did take photos and fingerprints, but he'd been in the water, medical examiner says for several days at least. All we know now is he's an unidentified deceased male. I sent what information we have to the National Crime Information Center. We'll see if they can match him up with a missing persons report. It may be a few days."

Shaken, I sat in silence. Bad enough the poor kid was dumped into the ocean, quite likely murdered. Then for no one to even know his identity. Not that long ago, he was someone's baby boy. I sighed.

"Yeah." Muñoz shifted. "So's how's everything in Arroyo Loco? I see you got new sidewalks."

"Indeed, we did. New bridge, new storm drains, new sidewalks. Lots of new neighbors, too. I've only just met some of them. As you know, the last few days of this last semester were a bit overwhelming. I missed several homeowners' meetings."

"Any interesting new neighbors?"

I wondered about Muñoz's concern with my new neighbors. "Why do you ask?"

"Just making conversation. You had a lot of vacancies out here. Just curious who's moved in."

I narrowed my eyes. His questions seemed like more than idle curiosity. I started enumerating on my fingers. "Well, no one too fascinating. Nina Arriaga is back in her house next door to the roadhouse. There's a new young couple in the Carper's place. They have several young boys. The Rosenblum's niece and her family have moved into that new house on their property where the fire happened. I've been hearing rumors Wally's old house has sold and is being remodeled."

26

"What about the big place up here?" He pointed toward the McMansion, perched at the very end of Arroyo Loco Road.

"Hmm. Yes, it does seem like I remember Amanita saying something about someone being in there. But I thought that place was going to be tied up in litigation for several more months. Maybe someone's renting? I sure haven't been home enough to see any moving trucks or unfamiliar cars going by. Why?"

"Just wondered," he said, standing to leave.

I waved as he backed out, and felt only mild curiosity when his car headed up the hill toward the McMansion instead of down toward the highway. He drove past headed downhill only a minute or two later, so I guess there really wasn't much to see up there.

"Yoo-hoo! Estela, are you in there?" Freda sang as she came into sight. One side effect of those brand new sidewalks was the increase in visitors walking from house to house. No longer afraid of being flattened by a speeding driver as she wandered around the curve, Freda could safely navigate the sidewalk. She was hard to mistake in her bright orange muumuu, rivaled in it's vividness only by the freshly applied color in her spiky hair. I'd recently learned that Freda enjoyed a semi-illustrious career in European theater before she settled in our quiet village. Finally, we had an explanation for her flair for the dramatic, including those painted-on eyebrows, giving her an expression of perpetual surprise.

I called back, and put my book down again. I had almost made it through the prologue this time before being interrupted.

"Your friend the detective, he came by to see you just now, yes?" she said. "And how is he doing?"

Wanting to derail that salacious tone in her voice, I replied, expressionless. "I found a dead body on the beach this morning, Freda. Muñoz is a homicide detective. He came by to ask me some questions."

"Oh, my!" She flapped a hand at her face and sank onto the flowered cushion so recently vacated by Muñoz. "Oh, dear me!"

"Sorry. I didn't mean to be so abrupt."

"Oh, dear, me. I'm sure you were upset. A dead body! *Mein gott*! What is the world coming to!"

"So anyway, that's what he was here about. How are you today, Freda?"

"*Gut, gut*, but really Estela, a body. You must be so upset!"

"I'm fine, Freda. I didn't even actually see it. The dogs found it. All I did was call the sheriff to come and get it."

Freda looked horrified as she gazed at Scout, now innocently curled up asleep. I couldn't imagine what she might be thinking, although I had said the dogs had found the body. Time for a change of subject.

"And to what do I owe the pleasure of your visit this afternoon, Freda?"

Her eyes focused back to me. "Oh, well, Estela. I wanted to ask you. There is something here, Estela. Something I would like you to look at." She rolled to her side in the chair and stretched a short, pale leg toward me. Pulling at the hem of her muumuu, she revealed one wrinkled knee. "See, right here?" She turned her leg over, pointing to the back of the knee. "See that?"

Giving as brief a glance as possible, I said, "What, Freda? I don't see anything."

"Right there. That bump there. Do you know? What is that?"

I glanced again, and maybe saw a tiny brown mole embedded in the chubby wrinkles. "I think it's just a mole, Freda. Why are you concerned?"

"Oh, but I saw on the internet, how to know the skin cancers. It said they come on the backs of the knees. So I checked and I found that. Do you think that is a skin cancer, Estela? You are a doctor, yes? What do you think?"

I laughed. "I am a psychotherapist, Freda. I could only diagnose you if you had a paranoid delusion or an anxiety disorder like hypochondria." Here I gave her an inquisitive look, hoping she would take the possibility of hypochondria into serious consideration. "I wouldn't know a skin cancer from ringworm."

"Ringworm! That is disgusting. Oh, do come here, doggy," she said as Shiner deposited a slobbery rubber ball near her foot. All of these humans passing through his screened porch this afternoon, and Shiner had not been able to persuade even one to throw his ball.

"Here, doggy," Freda said again. "What is this one's name, Estela?"

"Shiner," I told her, puzzled at her sudden attention to my dogs.

"Here, Shiner, that's a good boy." She pointed at her leg again, trying to draw the dog's interest. "Smell this, Shiner, right here."

Shiner politely stretched his snout toward her leg, then picked up the ball and thrust it at her.

"He's not smelling it, Estela. Does that mean it is not skin cancer? Dogs can smell skin cancer, you know? I saw that on the news."

I tried not to laugh. "Yes, I saw that too, but they have to be trained to alert to the smell of cancer cells."

"Your dogs cannot smell cancer?"

"Well, yes, of course they can smell a million smells on you. Dogs don't have to be trained to smell. But they do have to be trained to alert you when they smell the odor you want them to identify. And you have to be trained to recognize their alert signal. That takes a lot of training."

"Humph!"

"Really, Freda, if you are that concerned, maybe you should make an appointment with your doctor."

"You are no help at all, Estela!" She stood to leave.

"Wait, Freda. Do you know anything about someone living in the big house?" I pointed to the top of the hill, but everyone in Arroyo Loco knows what you mean when you say "the big house."

"I do believe there is someone there. Renters, perhaps? I see a black car going by a few times a day."

"So you don't know who it is, a name or anything?"

"No ... nothing like that. Did you ask Marla? She should know, yes? Because she collects the homeowner dues."

That was a good thought. As treasurer for the homeowners' association in Arroyo Loco, Marla Weisel would be the most likely person to know who paid the dues on that property. Sadly, Marla and I are not close. She would be unlikely to answer her phone if I called. Not to mention, that mean little dog of hers, Zero, bites. Maybe I'd just pass her contact information along to Muñoz and he could do the following up. After all, he was the one who was so interested.

CHAPTER FOUR

I guess the rumor had spread that I was at home, because in the middle of my thanking Freda for her bright idea, my screened door squealed open, and Helen stood there, filling the doorway and towering over Freda. Helen is a big woman, not fat, but big-boned with wide shoulders. She favors full-skirted dresses featuring large flowers. As I said previously, today's were blue.

Freda looked up at Helen. "Do not bother," Freda said. "Estela's dogs do not know how to smell cancer." With that, she flounced away, her muumuu flowing gracefully behind.

"What was that about?" Helen said.

"Don't ask. I'm not even sure I know."

Helen sprawled herself across the other end of the swing.

"Hello! What's this?" she said, lifting the binoculars from the end table. "Spy glasses? Really, Estela? Who are you spying on?" One thing about Helen, you can always trust her to jump to cynical conclusions.

"I'm not spying! I've decided to take up birding as a hobby."

"Really." Her tone clearly indicated she did not believe me for one second.

"Yes, and I'm going to keep a list, too, of all the species I see."

She put the binoculars to her eyes and scanned the undergrowth across the road. "I can't see a dad-blasted thing. How does this device work?"

With some misgivings, I showed her how to focus.

"Oh, yes, now I can see Bryce's carport. Say, where is Bryce's truck? The carport's empty."

"He took Alice to town for groceries. His dad can't drive anymore, you know, since that fall, and his mother never did drive, so now Bryce has to take Alice and Ernie everywhere. Bryce left his dog, Tippy, in our yard. That's how I know where they went."

"Cripes, Estela, that dog spends more time with your dogs than with Bryce." As we chatted, she continued to peer at the Bantam's house across the road and up a short hill from mine. "You know, probably it's a good thing Bryce never could get a job. Now he's free to take care of his parents. I am surprised he even has a driver's license."

I made no reply, as I wasn't so sure he did.

"If you ask me," she said, which I hasten to add I had not, "that kid has some kind of brain damage. Never worked a day in his life. Who gets away with that unless they've got some kind of serious disability?"

I raised my eyebrows, hoping that would be taken as a sufficient response to Helen's ill-supported observation. I am generally reluctant to diagnose psychopathology in someone who could just as easily be described as plain lazy.

"Whoo-ee, check it out," Helen said, waving at the other house. "There's Ernie on his porch." She took the binoculars down and looked at me. "Oh, I guess you can't see him, huh?" She put the glasses back to her eyes, all set to wave again at Ernie. "Aw, shucks, he's walking back inside."

It took a minute for her words to sink in. "What did you say?"

"I said he walked back inside. You missed him."

"He walked?"

"Yes. Oh. Yes, I see what you mean. He stood up and walked inside."

"So, Ernie, who no one has seen walk since he fell off that ladder and broke his leg last year, that Ernie, stood up and walked?"

"Yes. And he did it while his wife and son were gone and he thought no one could see him. You think Ernie is working some kind of insurance fraud thing? You know, to avoid going back to work?"

"Maybe. In any case, the fact that Ernie can walk seems like a piece of information we should keep to ourselves. Knowing that might come in handy sometime down the road."

"Who's this "we" kemosabe? I'm gonna use that juicy little tidbit first chance I get."

"Use it for what, Helen?"

"Now, don't get all worked up. I'm just saying, like you said. That information could come in handy someday. It's like a clue in a mystery." She went back to scanning with the binoculars. "What's that thing on the Bantam's porch railing up there. It looks like one of those mosquito-catching bugs only gigantic, with whirligigs on top?" She pointed in the general direction, but I knew what she was asking about.

"It's a drone. Bryce bought himself a drone last week. He's been learning to fly it"

"Well, what the heck is he going to do with that? Deliver packages? Spy on us?"

"So far, the only use he's found for it is to fly over my yard to check on Tippy."

"Well, that's just dandy. Pretty soon none of us will ever have to walk anywhere again. We'll just send our drones out instead. Criminy, I can almost read the lettering on the cereal box up there, Estela. These things are amazing." A long silence followed while Helen aimed the binoculars at various windows on this side of the Bantam's house. "Oh, yes. Yes, indeedy, I can see where you might get yourself into a whole lot of trouble with these things, Estela." She dropped the binoculars back onto the table as though they'd suddenly taken on a evil curse.

I could only agree, and resolved to focus in the future on strictly avian species. Helen picked up the notebook I'd left next to the binoculars, where I'd written the one bird I had been able to identify so far.

"Scrub jay," she read. "So this is your list? I see you've got a ways to go."

"I've only just started, Helen. Anyway, those jays chase all the other birds away. I think I might have seen a dusky-footed flycatcher. I need to get a book next time I'm in town."

"Honestly, I think you should have more than one bird on your list before you start calling yourself a birder. Anywho, I only came up to ask if you want to come to dinner tonight. Grant went sea-fishing with some buddies and hauled home a mess of stuff. Some of it I don't even recognize. There's one with these long tentacle-things with what looks like eyeballs on the ends. And another one has this ... this big nose? I figure I'll just slather it all with butter and herbs and let him grill the whole mess. He can chop it up while it's grilling so no parts are recognizable after it's cooked. It's too much food for the two of us."

"Gosh, Helen." On the one hand, I wanted to be gracious, and on the other ... ick. "That's very kind of you to invite me." What should I do here, go for the outright lie? The truth is, I am not the most adventurous person when it comes to food. Maybe I should take a chance for once? Would something I had to pry loose from my freezer really be more palatable than the promised "mess?" How could I refuse? I could offer to bring something to contribute and then eat mainly my own dish. Sadly, my culinary skills are widely recognized to be mediocre at best, and Helen would most likely turn down my offer.

In addition to eating something disgusting, I would also have to get home after dark. Lately Arroyo Loco has been having a serious invasion of wild boar. No one has been injured yet, but whole yards have been uprooted, and the sudden appearance of an ugly boar had forced more than one neighbor indoors at a greater rate of speed than they had moved in many years. I had no interest in meeting a boar several hundred feet from home and after dark.

For the moment, I went with a quick change in topic.

"Say, Helen, do you know anything about someone living in the big house?"

"I thought lawyers had that place all tied up in legal knots?"

"Yes, I did too, but apparently there is someone living there."

"Nope, don't know anything about it. While we're on the subject of neighbors, have you met Lauren's new friend?" Helen dipped her head in the direction of Lauren's house, out of sight around the curve.

"Is that the new friend with the lime-green Kia parked in Lauren's driveway most of the time? Seems like she's even there overnight these days."

"Oh, yes," Helen confirmed. "She's definitely there overnight."

"So, are they officially dating? I thought Lauren said she would never date again after the last one left her for an internet affair."

"Possibly they are not what you would call dating, but definitely keeping company."

"Keeping company? That's a tad archaic, isn't it? You and I are keeping company."

"Hardly, Estela! Are you nuts? I'm married! We are not keeping company."

"Calm down, Helen, there's no need to get testy." I crossed my eyes at her. "I only meant I haven't heard that expression in a long time. I think what the young people say these days is 'hooking up.'"

"Hooking up? That doesn't even make any sense." Helen gave a long sigh and heaved herself off the swing. "Well, Grant hooked up a bunch of something today and we're going to grill it. Are you coming to dinner?"

"Oh, thanks again, Helen, but I'd better stay here. I don't want to leave the dogs alone." What a lame excuse. It really is shameful how I use those dogs to get out of things I don't want to do anyway. Although, it is true that the dogs and I would be staying alone that night. What with all of the excitement that day, I really preferred to curl up with a bowl of ramen and my novel.

My godson Diego and his new wife Alex left yesterday on their long-awaited honeymoon, so the dogs and I were alone for the whole next week. Finding that body wasn't exactly giving me the creeps, but I left several lights on all evening, anyway. Helen's hulk of a husband, Grant probably would have walked me home, toting his shotgun, too. And I might have taken the dogs with me, but as I mentioned, Helen keeps cats.

Shiner and Scout have no desire to have their faces ripped off in an unprovoked cat attack.

Tuesday, and my second day of leisure dawned shrouded in the typical coastal June gloom. Somehow, the trip to dog beach had lost its usual appeal. I was scheduled to drop by my friend Inez Gabiola's sheep ranch sometime that day or the next to get instructions for watching over her sheep ranching enterprise while she and her prize-winning herding dog went off to a national trial to win even more ribbons and titles. My Shiner had won a few local ribbons, but we're not into the business seriously enough to be invited to national trials. Not that we wouldn't be if we focused more on sheepherding and less on earning a living and finding dead bodies.

The ranch hands would take care of Inez's stock while she was gone, and her busy dog day care business required its own caretaker, so I would only be responsible for sending Shiner out to the hills in the early evenings to bring the sheep down to the barn. That job cannot be accomplished without a trained dog.

Thinking I would go to the ranch after lunch, I strolled to the next house up the hill from mine, occupied by Amanita Warten. Part of the big house was visible from Amanita's porch. I could ask her if she knew anything about the people apparently now living there. Amanita and I are not the best of friends. Actually, the rest of us think Amanita doesn't have any friends. She's one of those people who marches into a room full of strangers and immediately tells them what to do and how to do it. It's funny how some people seem to know how to integrate themselves into a new group and be accepted and welcomed, and other people never learn that no matter how many times they fail.

Amanita stepped out her door at my knock, clearly not willing to admit me inside. Surprise and suspicion furrowed her brow.

"What do you want, Estela?"

"Good morning, Amanita," I chirped, trying not to sound too much like a nervous sparrow. Deciding to skip the small talk and get straight to the point, I said, "Someone said you might know the family living in the big house." I pointed, just to underscore my meaning. "Do you know their name? Or is anyone even living there?"

Amanita narrowed her eyes at me in suspicion. "What's it worth to you, Estela?"

"Oh, for pity's sake, Amanita, I'm just asking."

"Yes, but why? Those neighbors are my friends. You don't need to invite yourself to join us. They don't want any more friends."

Hmm. Every time I learned a new detail about these people, they seemed more mysterious. I wondered what sort of a person would be Amanita's friend. "Can you at least tell me their name?"

"No."

The conversation was making me a little hot under the collar. I stepped back, feeling the blood flushing my face. Amanita may have read my body language, because she relented for a moment.

"I can't tell you their name because I don't know it."

I thought this through. "You're friends with them, but you don't know their names?"

"Well, we might not exactly be friends. I did go up there once to invite them to a homeowners' meeting, and another time to ask them to come to a potluck supper. They have a gate, you know. You have to press the buzzer, then a voice comes on the speaker by the gate."

This was more like it. "So did you go inside? Is it a family living there? I haven't seen anyone at the meetings."

"Right. Well, one time no one answered. I could see them moving around in there, but no one answered."

"And the second time?"

"The other time the voice said to go away. I invited them, but they said 'go away' so I left."

Hmm. Some friends. However, as I've said, we don't think Amanita really has any friends, so maybe she's just unclear on the concept. "Okay, so no idea what their name is? They don't have their name by the mailbox or anything?"

"Their mailbox is on the wall down at the roadhouse like all the rest of ours, Estela."

"Oh, right. Good point."

Amanita puffed herself up the way she always did when she'd scored a point. "And it is a family," she finally added. "They have children, or at least teenagers. If you'd been watching, you would have seen two teenagers being driven to school and home. Or driving. The boy drives, you know. Or you would know if you paid any attention to our neighborhood." Somehow Amanita made it sound like not being a busybody was a personality flaw.

Possibly if I threw Amanita a bone, she might be more forthcoming. "You are a very observant person, Amanita."

She only narrowed her eyes at me again, and said, "Huh!" I think I might have gone a bit overboard with that last remark. She yanked open her screen, her intention to end the conversation obvious.

I gave her a weak wave and turned to go as she slammed inside. How could I find out who lived in that house? And why, again, did I need to know.

CHAPTER FIVE

I'd barely made it back to my porch before Muñoz's dented sedan rolled into my driveway again. He climbed out, waving a paper in my direction. A nice lightweight cotton suit today, in a pale gray, paired with a light blue dress shirt and tie. The shoes were a slightly darker shade of gray, and looked European. But then, what do I know about men's footwear? We settled onto the porch furniture. I offered coffee, but he declined. I know how much water and coffee to use, and I only buy fair trade shade-grown coffee and grind it myself. If the machine makes bad coffee, that can hardly be blamed on me.

"What's up, today?" I said.

"We got some information on that body." He smoothed his paper across one knee. "You have any luck identifying the occupants in that house up the hill?"

"Hold the phone here for a second. If you want my help, you need to tell me why you're asking about that family. Do they have something to do with the body on the beach? What's the story here? And who was that on the beach?"

Muñoz made serious eye contact and puffed out his cheeks, thinking. I waited. "Well, let me answer your second question first."

"Whatever."

"As I told you, the body is that of a young man, but no one has made any missing persons report anywhere in this vicinity."

"Yes, you said that. That's just terrible, I think. A young person goes missing and no one reports it? Where is his family? Someone must care about him."

"Okay, well, let me finish."

I sat back and shut my mouth.

"So, I got a phone call from an FBI investigator yesterday. A guy by the name of ...." He extracted his notebook from an inside pocket, flipped through a few pages and read. "Special Agent Roybal. He asked if we knew anything about the occupants of that house. Says a young man about the age of the body is a possible occupant. Have you learned anything?"

I stared at him, slowly shaking my head, "No." Then I remembered my conversation with Amanita. "Oh, wait. Amanita just told me there are two teenagers living there. That it's a family, and they have two teenagers."

"That fits."

"But if it was their child, why wouldn't they have reported him missing?"

Muñoz stared, expressionless. "Think about it. There could be a dozen reasons. They might think he's somewhere else. They might know he's gone, but aren't concerned."

"Oh, yes, because we're the ones who found a body. They don't know we found a dead guy. Maybe they just think he's at his summer job or some place like that."

My suggestions were interrupted by the detective's phone.

"Medical examiner's office," he muttered. He made the connection as he exited the porch, and conducted his conversation in the relative privacy of the driveway, walking in circles as he talked.

I used the break constructively, putting more effort into finding out what the neighbors might know about the mysterious family. I gave some thought to who the nosiest neighbors might be, figuring they would be the one's most likely to know anything, I dialed Bryce's number and waited while he answered with his full name. Very business-like. Wondered what line of business he was in.

"Hi, Bryce. Quick question. Do you know the name of the family living in the big house? They must be renting, huh? Just wondered if you know their name."

"I know they get a lot of traffic from suspicious-looking black cars with tinted windows, Estela."

"Hmm. I don't believe I've ever seen any suspicious black cars going past here."

"No wonder, Estela. You don't pay attention to anything going on around here. You missed another HOA meeting last week, you know."

Hard to decide how to respond to this, although in all fairness to Bryce, he was right. I had missed that darned meeting. "Okay, so ... and you don't know their name?"

"Ask Marla. She's the treasurer. She'd know who's paying their HOA dues."

"Good idea, Bryce. Don't know why I didn't think of that." Of course Freda had suggested that very thing yesterday, but I had failed to follow-up. I assured Bryce again that he'd had a brilliant idea. We disconnected.

Muñoz was back on the porch. "Any luck getting a name? 'Cause I'm telling you, there is something going on up there. FBI won't tell me what, or who. They'll only say there's a person of interest in that house."

"A person of interest in identifying the young man on the beach? Or some other case entirely?"

"Not sure. I think it is fair to assume a connection. Whichever it is, they don't have probable cause for a search warrant, and no one answers the gate when any of us rings. They're asking me who's living there, and not telling me why they want to know."

"You mean the FBI has been up there?"

"That's what they tell me."

"Hmm. Maybe that explains the mysterious black cars that have been cruising our canyon."

He raised his eyebrows. "Black cars?"

"Yes. Both Amanita and Bryce say black cars with tinted windows have been driving past on the way up there."

"Can you describe them?"

"Uh, no. I've never actually seen them." Anyway, I thought, didn't I just do that? "Do you think they could be the FBI?"

"Possibly." He shrugged. "All I know is, the FBI investigator is treating me and the whole sheriff's department like we're local yahoos, then asking for information. Did you talk to that woman who collects the dues?"

"Marla."

"Yeah, that Marla with the mean dog."

"That would be the one. I can give you her phone number and you can call her. I wouldn't recommend going over there." I tore a blank page out of my bird-list notebook, then had to go into the kitchen to get the phone number. Evidently I don't call Marla often enough to have memorized her number. Muñoz reached for the handset on the end table when I handed him the paper.

"Oh, well, no. You don't want to call on my landline either. Marla won't answer."

"She sees your number and she won't answer the phone?"

"'Fraid not."

He shook his head while punching the number out on his cell. After I realized Marla's display would now show the county sheriff's department, I wasn't surprised she didn't answer Muñoz's call either. It was always possible Marla was at work, or engaged in some other constructive activity, and not sitting around waiting for phone calls.

While Muñoz was leaving his message, I called Helen and asked her to give Marla a jingle. Helen is on better terms with Marla than most of the rest of us. Not sure why. I just know she is, and, as it turned out, Helen is on good enough terms to even have Marla's work number.

"Sure thing, 'Stel'," she said. "I'll get right back to you. Just one thing, though." I should have known I wouldn't get anything out of Helen without giving her information in return. "Why do you want to know?"

I decided to sit on as much information as I could. I'd already spilled the beans to Freda about finding a body on the beach, but I didn't need to say anything about a possible connection between the body and the family in the big house, or about the FBI's apparent interest. My lack of awareness about the latest neighborhood gossip is probably matched only by my unwillingness to contribute interesting tidbits, even when I had them.

"Oh, I'm not really sure. Muñoz is asking, and I told him you would be the expert at finding out." There that should do it. Ego-stroking never hurts.

I offered Muñoz some lunch while we waited to hear Helen's report, but again, he declined, jiggling his knee the way some guys do when they're anxious.

"So, what was that with the medical examiner's office? Did they have some news? And what's with that paper you were waving around earlier? Is that body connected to the family or not?" I shuddered with the next thought. "Do you really think that could be their son?"

I felt comfortable asking for this information since, as of last month, I had signed a contract to become an official consultant with the sheriff's department. I did not feel so comfortable asking if I was on the time clock for this investigation yet, or if we were just having an amiable chat.

"Preliminary results show a small amount of water in the lungs," he said, smoothing the paper over his knee again and reading out loud. "Not consistent with drowning. Odds are, the victim was not breathing when his body was dumped."

"What the heck does that mean? He breathed in water, but he didn't drown? That's very confusing."

The detective grunted his agreement.

I was trying to picture how someone could have water in their lungs, but not enough to drown. We've all had a swallow that went, as they say, down the wrong way. Was it something like that? "Did someone stick his head under water, but then let him up before he drowned? Does he show any other signs, like blunt force trauma to the head, or bruises on the neck to indicate strangulation? Young healthy people don't just drop dead. How was this kid killed?"

"Medical examiner does not see any other signs of trauma anywhere on the body."

"Hmm. So the victim was ferried out to sea after being killed, method unknown, dumped overboard, and then washed back in with the tide?"

Muñoz regarded me with a lowered brow.

"What?" I said.

"You're making a lot of assumptions there, Dr. Nogales. You found the body on the beach. Did it wash in with the tide? We don't know for sure. I mean, we might make that assumption, but we don't know for sure."

"You think someone left it there, all wet and soggy like that? And in a pile of other stuff that washed in with the tide?"

"Could have happened. You're also assuming the victim was dead before being loaded onto a boat."

"And you think the victim was killed on the boat?"

"Don't know. Just saying, we don't know. We don't know if there was even a boat."

I thought about this. He was right, of course. Taking everything into consideration, I'm always going to go for the easy answer, the one that requires the fewest convolutions, the least number of assumptions. "Fair enough," I said. My phone rang, Helen's name in the display.

"Marla doesn't know the renter's name," Helen said. "Some property management company in San Mateo sends the check for the HOA dues every month." She recited the name and number while I scribbled it down, trying not to transpose anything. "That what you want?"

"That should do it, Helen. Thanks so much."

"No problem. You know, Estela, you could make more of an effort to get to know Marla. She's usually not that bad a person."

A few scenes from my past encounters with Marla flashed through memory. "Yes," I said, "I'm sure you're right. I'll think about that." Not! I thanked her again, and hung up.

Muñoz strolled back out to the driveway to call the property managers, again protecting his privacy, or at least his behavior was a sign that I was not on the payroll on this case ... yet. He was back in a flash.

"She said the family's name was none of my business," he announced when he returned. "Without probable cause or a warrant, 'that information is not available.'"

"Hmm. Would it be available to the FBI?"

"That is an excellent question," he said, moving toward the door again. "Better pass this information along to that Agent Roybal." With a puff of black smoke from the exhaust pipe, Muñoz drove away. Looked like that old sedan was preparing to break down again, and sooner rather than later.

I sat down to puzzle on the situation. Some people call this meditation. I call it staring absently into space. I let my mind wander.

One of the most annoying aspects of living in a place like Arroyo Loco is that everyone along our meandering lane seems to know everything about everyone else here. You drive home with your car windows blocked by pallets of toilet paper and gigantic boxes of detergent and, in a blink, everyone knows you've been shopping at the discount warehouse. You try to roll silently home in the wee hours, and by the next Saturday morning coffee klatch, everyone in town knows you have a new beau. Not that I've ever done that. I had some of our younger residents in mind with that thought.

Surely in a community like this, where folks pay attention to everyone else's business, someone must know who is living in the big house. I just haven't tried hard enough to find out what my neighbors know. I poured the last of the coffee into my adult version of a Tommy Tippy cup, black and gray instead of pink or blue, but still with a snap-on lid and slot to sip through. I left the dogs safely fenced in their yard, and headed downhill on the freshly formed sidewalk to ask around.

It was Tuesday, and we have quite a few new neighbors who are young enough to be off at work or school this afternoon. The new house on the property where the Rosenblums used to live looked empty, with Jeannie, Josh and their youngsters off for the day. The children had been allowed to stamp their tiny handprints in the concrete while it was wet. Their names and a date had been inscribed beside the prints. An even smaller print of a cat's paw, claws extended, nestled between the children's prints.

Next door, Delia and her kids were away, but across the street, Freda sat snapping string beans on her front porch. I wandered to her steps and explained my mission. She set the bowl beside her chair, and we walked together to Helen's. According to Freda, Helen had taken early retirement from her job as the librarian at the state men's prison after her recent marriage to Grant. She was going to let him be the breadwinner and relax to the relative leisure of a housewife, at least until boredom set in.

After collecting Helen, the three of us walked across the bridge and as far as Sunshine Rainbow's house, shared with her friend, Raymond Watts, who was nowhere in sight. We settled in on their porch. Sunshine is our resident psychic, a holdover from the sixties, but she also often has plain-spoken, down-to-earth advice about the latest crisis in Arroyo Loco.

I suggested calling Nina, living one more house downhill, to join us. Instead, Freda popped up and bustled over to Nina's to ring her bell. The two of them were back five minutes later, both bearing fragrant cups of what was probably Nina's usual high-end coffee. I should remember, there is always a purpose behind Freda's friendly spirit.

Once everyone had found a spot, been offered and in some cases accepted a tall glass of iced tea, and the health and well-being of everyone present had been inquired into, I was given time to explain what I needed from them. I tried to frame my description of the situation so that it would come across as a generous sharing of numerous juicy bits of gossip. Although all were happy to ooh and aah over my news about the body, no one there had any idea who the people living in the big house were either, even though almost everyone reported having seen the black cars going by.

My request for information wavered when I was unable to provide a clear and convincing reason why we should care who lived in that house, especially as long as the HOA dues were being regularly paid.

It is possible I was supposed to keep my lips zipped about the FBI's interest in the people in that house. I couldn't exactly remember what Muñoz had said about that. On the other hand, the general chatter was threatening to drift into gossip about Lauren's new girlfriend if I didn't reel it back in quickly.

"So," I said, "it turns out it's the FBI who really wants to know who's living in that house." This was followed by a hushed silence.

CHAPTER SIX

"*Dios mio!*" Nina said. "Seriously? The Federal Bureau of Investigation wants to know?"

"Oh, brother!" Helen sighed. "Not another criminal in Arroyo Loco!"

"Perhaps it is those FBI men driving in those black cars?" Freda said. Several of us nodded, but Helen disagreed.

"They can't all be FBI cars. Some of them have really tinted windows, and anyway, there are too many to all be FBI. Cripes, they go past my house two, three, sometimes four times a day!"

I couldn't believe I'd never seen even one of these cars. Maybe I really have gotten out of touch with the neighborhood. "Imagine that," I said, "and no one has any idea who's in those cars?"

"Well, 'Stel' how would we know? You can't see in the windows. They're tinted!"

"That is right, 'Stel'," Freda said, mimicking Helen. "We would have to stop them if we wanted to look inside."

"Amanita says there's a whole family living there, including two teenagers who get driven back and forth to school," I said.

"Oh, so perhaps it is only the family that has black cars with tinted windows." Freda said. "We could stop them and invite them to our coffee klatch."

"Good idea," Helen said. "Let's stop one of them, look inside, and ask them who they are. This is our street. We can be Nosy Parkers if we want. We can stop them."

"*Es verdad*," Nina muttered, "but how?"

"Easy peasy," Helen said, waving in wide gestures. "Turning in here off the highway, they're usually going pretty fast, and like everyone, they gun it going uphill and across the bridge, but when they're coming downhill, they slow way down and even stop before turning onto the highway. We just stand out in the road and stop them, make up some excuse, chat about something, then look inside. Like I said, easy as pie!"

Freda looked confused. "Pie is not that easy, Helen. What are you talking about?" English is not Freda's first language, and she can often be confused by common idioms.

"Trust me, Freda, I could stop them," Helen assured her. "The trouble is, I don't want to be standing around all afternoon waiting for a black car to come cruising downhill."

"Yes," I agreed. "What we need is some kind of an early warning system."

"That's the ticket!" Helen said. "Here's an idea, 'Stel', you sit out on your porch—you're always out there anyway—and you be on the lookout for a car coming downhill. Then you text me, and I get out on the road in time to stop them."

"Wouldn't it be better if Estela called me, and I stopped them?" Sunshine asked. "I mean, after all, I live closer to the stop sign at the highway, and would have more time to get out in the street."

Few of us could disguise our skepticism about this plan. In her multi-colored broom skirt, flowing silver mane, and Birkenstock sandals, Sunshine's status as an aging hippie is obvious. The image of Sunshine dashing into the road in that get-up to stop a black sedan with mysteriously tinted windows was amusing, but maybe not a workable plan. On the other hand, what alternative did we have?

I nodded, lost in thought. It seemed like a plan, but the little voice in my head that kept saying "What could possibly go wrong?" had me worried.

"*No te preocupe*, Sunshine, don't worry." Nina said. "We'll run out together and stop the car."

"Okay, then!" Helen said. "It's a go! 'Stel', you head on up the hill and the rest of us will be ready to go when we get the signal."

"Ooh, yes!" Freda was bouncing and clasping her hands tightly with excitement. "We will be ready! Wait ... what is the signal again, please?"

"I'll call Sunshine, Freda," I said, "or someone, and then we'll all call each other."

"And when we get the call," Helen added, "we run into the road and stop the car."

I had my doubts, but they all seemed so eager. "Okay, I'm off for home now, and I'll be ready to send the signal." As I walked, I considered the possible dangers of our plan. If the black car did belong to the FBI, the danger would probably be minimal. Unless someone got careless and stepped too close to the moving vehicle. If the car belonged to someone else, the situation could get more complicated. What sort of a person typically drives a black car with tinted windows? Maybe I should wait until I see the car, and decide then whether I should call anyone.

I didn't have long to wait. In fact, I had barely gotten across the bridge when the nose of a black sedan appeared around the curve. I turned and waved frantically at my friends still gathered on Sunshine's front porch, hollering for all I was worth. "Hey! Hey, here it comes!"

Much faster than you would imagine a woman of that age could move, Freda came flying off the porch and pumped toward the middle of Arroyo Loco Road, today's green muumuu flying. Made of solid Austrian stock, Freda never hesitates to join in a fray. She was followed in an only slightly less hurried way by Helen and Sunshine. Nina stepped more sedately as far as the sidewalk. She waited there as the car approached, smiling in a friendly and welcoming manner.

I, of course, was still standing at the end of the bridge where the car would pass within a few feet. Discretion always being the better part of valor, I eased behind a tree trunk at the end of the Smutts' driveway and pretended to be engrossed in surveying the creek below. What with all of my waving and yelling, I had probably already been spotted by the occupants of the vehicle, but I wasn't going to draw any more attention to myself than necessary. The car slid silently past. Only then did I slip out and trot along the sidewalk to catch up.

My friends had formed a gaggle of a roadblock, and Helen flagged the car to a stop by waving the skirt of her bright red dress. The black car drew close, slowed, and stopped. By the time I got to where I could see anything, Sunshine and Helen were engaged in light banter with the driver, while Freda peered through the open window into the darkness inside the car. She batted her eyelashes coquettishly at someone inside. Nina's view was, like mine, from the rear of the car. She had her lipstick out and was writing discreetly on the tiny mirror with a brilliant shade of mauve.

What with all of them in the way, I couldn't see much, especially with the rear windows so heavily tinted. I did hear a friendly and accented male voice say, "Pleasure to meet you ladies," just before the windows rolled up and the car slid forward again toward the highway.

54

"Ooh, Estela!" Freda scurried across to me, her hands shaking in excitement. "Did you see? So handsome! I think those guys were mobsters, just like on tv! Don't you think, Helen?"

"Oh, yeah," Helen said, cocking one eye at Freda. "Very handsome. Especially the schnoz on that one guy. I think you're right about the mobster part, though. They were crime family for sure." Given Helen's experience working in the state prison, her opinion on the subject carried somewhat more weight than you might ordinarily expect. On the other hand, I wondered, how does one identify members of a crime family on sight?

"How do you know, Helen?"

"Well, for one thing," she said, "they waved at us. We thought at first they might be FBI agents, but when they waved, I knew they weren't. You never see FBI agents wave like that. Federal agents take life way too seriously. Agents would never have waved at us."

Hmm. Revising my judgement about how seriously to take Helen's opinions.

"And didn't you see, Estela?" Sunshine said. "They had on black dress shirts with silver ties, black hair slicked back, dark glasses." She gave a pretend shiver with her shoulders. "Extremely mob-like."

"Hmm, sounds like mobsters to me," I agreed. Mobsters from a movie, maybe, but I didn't say that part out loud.

"And their suits," Freda added. "Did you see? Shiny, like black shark-skin suits? Bad guys for sure."

This caught Sunshine's animal-rights activists' attention. "Shark-skin! Real shark-skin? That's terrible! Those really were bad guys!"

I put my hand on her shoulder. "No, Sunshine, I think Freda was referring to the kind of fabric. Their suits weren't made of the skin from real sharks." A change of subject seemed in order. "So, did you find out anything about who's living up there? Those guys were certainly friendly enough with you."

"Oh, yeah, very charming," Helen said. "I mean, within the context of they were definitely mafioso. They even had the thick-accent-thing going on."

"You mean Italian accents?"

"*Nein*, not Italian," Freda said. I was inclined to take Freda's word for that.

Helen's brow furrowed. "Not Italian. More like, eastern."

"You mean Jersey?"

"No, not New Jersey." She scowled at me, not appreciating the joke. "Eastern European, possibly Russian?"

I gave Helen a long skeptical look. "You are able to discern an eastern European accent, and distinguish a Russian accent from, say a Kazakhstani accent or a Polish one?"

"Who do you think we have filling up the cells in that prison these days, 'Stel'?"

"Oh." I'd never thought about that. Helen probably had a good point. I flipped my eyebrows up and down in reply and tried to steer the conversation in a different direction.

"Did they at least tell you the family's name?"

"Yeah, we asked," Helen said. "They said 'Ragazzo, Bravo Ragazzo.'" Even as she spoke, her head was motioning, no, her short hair swaying.

"The family's name is Ragazzo?" I rolled this over in my mind. Never heard it before. It sounded vaguely Italian, but what did I know?

"When I asked who was living up there, the driver said some other word, in like, Turkish or another language, then 'Bravo Ragazzo,' and then they laughed. I guess that was the name. Either that, or someone in the car is a Martin Scorsese fan." She didn't sound convinced. We'd wandered back to the sidewalk by then.

"Did anybody notice anything else?" Helen asked.

Freda had something to contribute. "The other one, the one in the passenger seat? He was so young. And very cute. You should have come and met him, Estela." She leered.

"I have something else," Nina said, flashing her lipstick case around.

"What the ...?" Helen squinted at the tiny mirror.

"It's the license plate number." Nina said. "That could come in handy, right?" She looked at the mirror. "Except I'd better get this written down somewhere quick. I think that last number's already smeared." She and Rainbow hurried up the porch to find paper and pencil.

Something about what Freda had said about the passenger had me wondering. "When you say the passenger was young, Freda, did you mean he was young enough to be the teenage son in the family?" If the passenger was the teenage son, I puzzled, then who was the body on the beach?

"*Nein*, not that young," Freda said. "Not a child. And he was wearing a suit, too. He was perhaps thirty or forty years old?"

I nodded. Young is a relative term. "Well, thanks for trying," I said. "If those guys were not FBI, and we know the FBI has been driving up there, at least now we know there's not just one black car."

"Here's that license number." Nina handed me the tiniest piece of paper I may have ever seen. I slid it carefully into the watch pocket on my shorts, the only place it would not have immediately gotten lost.

"Okay, so this was useful," Helen said. "Should we do this again the next time you see a car coming this way?" This question resulted in a burst of conversation. The chattering sounded like it could go on for a while. I extricated myself from the group and took a few steps toward home.

Rainbow called out, "We'll let you know if we need you to signal again."

I waved my acknowledgment and hurried home. The dinner hour was upon me. What with all of the excitement, I couldn't remember if I had even had lunch.

At home, on my computer, I discovered that bravo ragazzo means something like "good guy" in Italian. Thus, a question arose. Did the men in the car really give us the name of the family living in the house, or were they telling us the family were nice people? Or, since they were saying it in Italian, maybe they were just making a joke at our expense. Should I tell Muñoz we finally had the name, or wait and see if he could get the name from another source?

I yawned. That was enough for one day. I called Inez to explain I would be at the ranch for my instructions the next afternoon and took myself and my novel off to bed. My intention is always to read myself to sleep. Most of the time, I drift off before accomplishing much in the reading department. Then, the next time I open the book, I'm lost. Characters I don't remember are engaged in activities that have no context, and I have to start over, re-reading the same pages I read the night before.

Wednesday morning I carried the binoculars and bird list out to the porch along with a bowl of whole grain cereal. After scarfing the cereal before it got soggy, I listened for birds, but did not hear any. Maybe it was too early. More likely too late. I focused the binoculars down the road, more out of boredom than anything, and spotted that lime-green Kia in Lauren's driveway. Definitely something going on there. So distracted I almost missed it, the sound of a car coming uphill caught my attention. One of those black cars cruised uphill around the curve and passed my porch. I dropped the binoculars just before it drew even with the porch, and held very still, hoping whoever was in that car would not notice me sitting there spying on my neighbors.

There was only the driver inside, and he didn't look my way. Must have been returning from dropping the kids at school, I thought.

As the car disappeared up the road, my phone rang, Muñoz's name in the display.

"Got a name on that family," he said. "Not sure, though. Odam?" Sounded like he was reading it. "Yaxshi Odam?"

"Hmm. That's not the name we got here, so I'm not sure." There was a long moment of silence. I could almost hear Muñoz wondering how I got a name, and why I hadn't called him when I did.

"What name did you get?"

"Uh, something Italian, but I'm not sure it's a name. Bravo Ragazzo?"

Muñoz mumbled to himself for a moment. "Uh, huh." More mumbling. "Any idea what kind of a name this Yaxshi Odam might be?"

Yaxshi Odam. I navigated to my favorite translation site on the laptop. "Can you spell that?" Typed in the letters as the detective read them off. "According to my computer, those are Uzbeck words meaning 'good guys.'" Funny coincidence. Someone was almost certainly pulling our collective legs.

"Uzbeck?"

"Yes, you know, from Uzbeckistan. I think that's in eastern Europe. Or maybe it's western Asia. I'd have to look that up."

"So these are good guys from Uzbeckistan? Or is that the last name?

"That I don't know. Where did you get your information and what do they say?"

Muñoz went on as though I had not asked. "Odam. Family name probably is Odam, and now we've got an tentative identification on the boy. Local high school has two students, a Sissy Odam and a Chip Odam. Neither one of them has been in school since at least last Thursday. Chip is nineteen years old. Senior. Enrolled six weeks ago. Record of poor attendance. Lives with both parents on Arroyo Loco Road."

"Well, Amanita says a boy lives in that house, but what connects this Chip to the body on the beach?"

"Matches description, plus the body has a lunch pass from that school in his back pocket. I said tentative identification."

I mumbled something affirmative-sounding. Still taking in the death of such a young person.

"Plus, we have no other missing persons. Possibly the body could have been brought here from someplace else. This is just more reasonable." Reasonable explanations always appeal to Muñoz.

"I get it. So now we have to find this Chip, or find out if he's missing. What's next?" I must be developing some psychic skills. I could almost hear Muñoz wondering what I meant by "we." Guess I should have waited for an official invitation before providing any consultation-like advice. On the other hand, he had called me.

"I have to get the family to let me in," he said.

Might have been my imagination, but it sounded like he emphasized the "I."

He continued. "Explain the situation. Find out why they haven't reported him missing. Try to get a confirmation of the identity."

"Yes, maybe it's not even their son. Chip might be visiting his grandmother or something."

I got the skeptical silence again. Then, "So, are you saying you want to come with me? There's definitely something hinky going on there. An educated set of eyes and ears might be a good idea. You'd be on the clock. Pick you up after lunch?"

Theoretically, I was supposed to be relaxing this summer, catching up on my reading, learning to identify birds. But a visit to the odd family in the big house sounded like way more fun. I spent the rest of the morning picking up dog toys, vacuuming, and catching up on the laundry, and was ready to go at the appointed time. I had even changed into more professional attire, and run a comb through my typically unruly curls.

CHAPTER SEVEN

A well-marked county sheriff's department SUV pulled up about twenty minutes later. I wondered if Muñoz's battered sedan had bitten the dust again, but a uniformed deputy sat at the wheel of the SUV, so probably Muñoz only wanted the visit to appear more official.

"Guess you're going in fully visible this time, huh?"

"Yeah. Didn't get a response last time I rang the bell. Thought this might work better."

I climbed into the back seat, behind the screen, for the short trip. This being Arroyo Loco, it was inevitable that one or another neighbor would be watching. I just hoped no one would start spreading rumors that I'd been arrested.

Muñoz used our brief ride to explain what I should look for, and to warn me he would be asking a few questions that might seem irrelevant to the investigation about the body on the beach. The deputy pulled directly in front of the front gate to the McMansion, and he went to the keypad on the post carrying a convincing passel of legal-sized papers. Looked very authoritative. Muñoz and I waited behind.

To my surprise, the buzzer was answered immediately and, after a brief explanation conducted via the tiny speaker on the post, the three of us were admitted inside the fence. A tall, broad-shouldered man with no hair, pocked skin, and a bulbous nose opened the door when we approached. If his tight sharkskin suit and firmly knotted narrow tie was any way to judge, his fashion sense was a little dated. Or possibly mobsters' fashions are more perennial than are the rest of ours.

Muñoz was able to convince him that we needed to step inside and speak to both Mr. and Mrs. Odam about their son, Chip. The tall man did not bat an eye at the use of those names. I could only conclude he had indeed been kidding around with my friends by giving them the name Bravo Ragazzo.

He admitted us to an entry room, asked us to wait there, and disappeared through a doorway. The only furniture in the large foyer was a low credenza. Even faint sounds echoed off the marble floor and empty walls. I thought about stepping to the doorway to try to see other parts of the house, but I didn't want to get caught snooping. Anyway, we were quickly joined by a much shorter and stockier man, also in a shiny suit, with thin, slicked-back hair. We had apparently interrupted this man's meal, because he tugged a cloth napkin from under his multiple chins before greeting Muñoz in a gravely voice.

"Mr. Odam?" Muñoz said, holding out his right hand.

Odam looked to the side and down as he dropped his napkin on the credenza. A slight smirk flitted across his face, disappearing as fast as it had appeared. Whatever he said next was going to be a lie. All the classic signs were there.

"Yes," he said, shaking Muñoz's hand. Totally lying, possibly about his name, possibly about something else, but his lie was given away by the obvious tell.

At that moment, we were joined by a woman, almost as short, equally well-dressed, with a coif that looked stiff enough to have withstood a missile attack. Both were in their mid-forties, shiny shoes, thin lips, and shifty, distrustful eyes. It could have been allergies, but the woman's blotchy red face said she'd been crying. Not your usual relaxing-at-home couple.

We enjoyed a brief round of introductions during which I was described as "a consultant." Odam didn't settle for that.

"And who is this pretty little lady?" he asked in a smarmy tone, a smile curling his lip. Muñoz gave him a long serious stare. Without altering his expression, Muñoz made eye contact with me, again for a few seconds too long, then turned back to Odam, pointedly ignoring the question. I was guessing Muñoz had never paid much attention before to how women are treated in such settings.

I let the detective do the talking, using my time and keen powers of observation to scope out the scene and do quick personality assessments of the two adults.

"Mr. Odam, Mrs. Odam, do you know the whereabouts of your son?" Muñoz asked, getting right to the point. "I believe he is known as Chip."

The Odams hemmed and hawed. The mother assured us that Chip was in school while the father shook his head, either denying the likelihood of that, or possibly in disgust that the boy could not be found in school. Again.

I scanned the foyer in which we all stood. The ceiling soared overhead where the curving stairs disappeared. Two arches opened, one to the right, one left. I could only catch glimpses beyond the openings, but all appeared to be without furniture or rugs. Maybe the family lived mostly upstairs. The wide carpeted treads curved to the left, providing access to the floor above. Movement caught my gaze and a set of girlishly-clad feet appeared on an upper step. Someone was sitting there listening in on our conversation.

"We really have no idea where you might find Chip at the present time, officer," the father said. "He is an adult, at least in age. We do not try, so much, to keep track of him any longer. He does what he wants." Mr Odam did not seem too pleased with this aspect of parenting.

"I understand," said Muñoz, the tone in his voice indicating that he did not. "I am sorry to have to tell you this, but I'm here because we have located the body of a young man, and there is the possibility that it may be that of your son. It may also be someone else. Do you have a photograph or two of Chip that I might have for identification purposes? At least one with him smiling, if you could, please."

That gave me a start. I hadn't seen the face of the body, of course. Was it possible it had been grinning? Holy *caramba*, you sure don't see that on television. Mrs. Odam's eyes widened, possibly thinking the same thing, and she looked at her husband. He resumed his oily smile. After a moment, he seemed to realize his wife was looking to him for direction. He said something to her, curt, and in a language I couldn't begin to identify.

She murmured something noncommittal, turned and started up the stairs to some other part of the massive house, presumably in search of photos of her son.

Muñoz watched her go, then turned back to Mr. Odam. "How about your daughter?" He glanced at his notebook. "Sissy, is it? Do you have any idea where we might find her this afternoon?"

"Umm, no, or, she should be on her way home from school. That is, if she went today. No, I really don't know at exactly this moment. Keeping track of the children is really more my wife's responsibility." Mr. Odam gave a weak smile that went no farther than his mouth and shrugged. He shifted and addressed me. "Women are better suited, you understand, to looking after the children. They have the child-care chromosomes and instinct. It is all very scientific ..." He continued talking, even after I had tuned out of his mansplaining. I didn't say anything, but I'm fairly certain my teeth were audibly grinding.

I watched as the pink flip-flops with plastic flowers drew back on the tread above, then disappeared. Muñoz caught my glance and I shot a look up the stairs. He nodded that he'd gotten the hint.

"Uh-huh," he said, turning back to Mr. Odam. "Well, we can wait until we've identified the young man, but we will need to talk to everyone who lives here, if it should turn out .... Well, let's get that identification done first."

Mrs. Odam reappeared, spikey heels first down the stairs, and offered Muñoz a snap-shot sized photo. He fumbled in a jacket pocket and came up with a cellophane evidence bag. Opening it, he. let Mrs. Odam drop the photograph inside before he looked at it. His furrowed brow indicated it wasn't quite what he had been hoping to see. I thought he should be grateful to get any kind of a paper photograph, these days.

"No school photos?" he asked.

Mrs. Odam shot a nervous glance at Mr. Odam and waited for him to answer.

"No, no school pictures. We've only just moved here."

"So, Chip doesn't have a dentist here either?"

Again, a negative response.

"How about a dentist where you lived before?"

"No, I do not believe so," Mr. Odam answered without consulting his wife. So much for the wife being in charge of the children's affairs.

Mrs. Odam looked puzzled. "What has this to do with a dentist?"

Muñoz looked at Mr. Odam and transferred his weight to the other foot. This was already an awkward conversation. The

66

appearance of Mrs. Odam's face, including smeared pancake make-up, indicated that she had spent a fair amount of time crying already today. "The dentist is for identification purposes," Muñoz reiterated.

Mrs. Odam did not appear any less confused. She leaned in and pointed at the photograph. "See, he's smiling here?"

Muñoz grunted and handed the envelope to me. I took a good long gander. It showed the head and shoulders of a young man slouched against a stucco wall. Possibly it had been taken in front of this very house. My first impression was that the boy in the photograph might be about to be the unfortunate victim of a firing squad. My second thought was that the picture resembled nothing so much as the type of photograph one might have taken to obtain a passport. Not exactly a casual family snap-shot. I handed the envelope back.

"I see." Muñoz nodded, looking again at the photograph. He clicked his pen, ready to make another notation. "And where did your family move here from, Mr. Odam?"

For the briefest second, Mr. Odam flashed narrowed eyes at us. By the time Muñoz looked up, the expression was gone.

"Is that really relevant, officer? We don't even know if your body has anything to do with our family. And really, knowing Chip as I do, I strongly suspect he has merely run off for a few days." The guy sure didn't seem to be too upset about the possibility that his young son might, at this very moment, be lying dead in the medical examiner's office.

There was a pause while Muñoz considered his response. "Fair enough," he said, "but I need you both to come with us to see if you can make an identification."

Mrs. Odam blanched and swayed slightly. Instead of comforting her, Mr. Odam tightened his jaw. Fresh tears slid down Mrs. Odam's cheeks, and she swiped at them with the napkin her husband had dropped on the credenza.

"Really, I am quite busy at the present time, officer, and you have the photograph. Is it not possible to see your body is not Chip from that photograph?"

"No, that's not possible, Mr. Odam. I need you to come to the medical examiner's office now, and try to make the identification."

Mr. Odam huffed in exasperation. "Very, well. We can come later this afternoon. Please, if you'll write that address down, we'll come this afternoon."

"No, sir," Muñoz persisted. "I need you to come now. I can provide a ride in our vehicle, and return you here afterwards."

"Really, I don't see why my poor wife needs to see your dead body!"

"I need both of you to make the identification. I'll also need DNA samples from each of you. My deputy can take those here." Even I knew that was unusual, under the circumstances. That must have been what Muñoz meant when he warned me he would be asking some strange questions.

"Absolutely not!" Mr. Odam barked. "We are not criminals!"

Muñoz stared back for the briefest of seconds, then said, "Of course not, Mr. Odam. Again, this is strictly for purposes of identification. I do need you to come with me now, though. I can get an unmarked vehicle, if you would prefer." Muñoz reached for his phone. He was becoming a broken-record, each time a bit more insistent. He turned to Mrs. Odam with sympathy, "Ma'am, you won't need to see the actual body. We can make a probable identification from photographs."

Without otherwise moving, Odam turned his head and barked an order in some foreign language toward another part of the house. This time it did sound eastern European to me.

His call got an immediate response in the form of the scrapping of chair legs across a hard floor.

"Yes, sir?" came from another room.

"Bring the car around. Now." Scowling at Muñoz, Mr. Odam said, "We will follow you in our own car."

As the others began to move in direction of the front door, I leaned just slightly to my left, trying to catch at least a glimpse of some other part of the house. What I saw at the other side of a large dining room was a white baby-gate stretched across the opening to what could have been a kitchen. Filling the opening above the gate was the drooling head of a silent black and tan bullmastiff. Had to be well over one hundred pounds of dog standing there. Generally, I like dogs. This one wasn't giving the impression the feeling was mutual. I scurried toward the front door. At the last minute, that napkin caught my eye. After wiping her tears, Mrs. Odam had dropped it back on the credenza. Surely, that napkin would be loaded with DNA, maybe even the DNA of both parents, right? I don't carry handy evidence bags around in my pocket, so had to be content with pincering the napkin up with two fingers to ferry it out to the deputy's vehicle.

"Here," I said, offering it to Muñoz once we were settled inside.

"What's this?"

"It's that napkin. The one Odam was using? And then Mrs. Odam wiped her nose on it?"

He opened another evidence bag and I dropped the napkin inside.

"It must have DNA on it, right?"

Muñoz held the bag up and looked inside. "Possibly. It's a cloth napkin."

"Is that bad? Does that mean it wouldn't carry DNA?"

"Sure, it would," he said. He glanced at the deputy. "It's only, the Odams are going to be short one napkin from their set." This seemed to be of some concern to Muñoz.

I nodded slowly, wondering about his priorities.

"Since we didn't have permission to collect it, we won't be able to use the evidence in court, but it could really help us figure out just who these people are. So ... good work."

I was riding in the back seat again. Muñoz thought it wouldn't be a good idea to let me out at my house with the Odam's and their employees in the car behind us. It would be better, he said, not to let them know I lived nearby. So I was along for the ride to the county medical examiner's office whether I wanted to go or not.

CHAPTER EIGHT

The Odam's black car, driven by the guy who had answered the door, pulled up behind us. I couldn't help but notice that Mr. Odam opened a rear door and stepped in, leaving his wife to teeter to the far side on her pointy heels and open her door herself.

We started off. I scrunched down to where even the top of my head was below the sill. No sense in giving the neighborhood more to talk about than they already had. Muñoz eased around to look over his shoulder.

"So, learn anything?" he said to me.

"Yes. Odam's lying."

"About what?"

"Almost everything, as near as I could tell. Odam is not his name, for starters. And if that woman is really his wife, he doesn't care a whit about her. And there is a young girl, close to Sissy's reported age, in that house. I saw her, or at least her feet. And I think, just based on reading the cues, I think Odam knows who that body is, but he doesn't care that much. Or at least he's not surprised the kid is dead. He's so unconcerned, I almost wonder if the kid is even his son."

We rode in silence for the remainder of the five-mile trip to the freeway on-ramp. There we merged into the flow of traffic and approached the steep downhill grade leading into town, the black car trailing us by a sedate distance. As I watched, a second black car pulled in behind the first one, also keeping some space between them.

"Hey," I said to Muñoz, "who's that in the second black car? The one behind the Odams?"

Muñoz turned and looked. "Beats me." He fussed with his phone as we crested the grade and started down. Looking back again, he said, "Might be FBI. Now we've flushed the Odam's out of that house, possibly the FBI hopes to question them. I've texted to ask, but I'm not getting an answer here."

I watched, but the two black cars maintained the distance between them, both following us.

"So, I have a couple of questions," I said, "although I'm not entirely sure I want to hear the answers. Why did you ask Mrs. Odam for a picture of Chip where he's smiling? Is the body smiling?"

Muñoz was absorbed in his phone, distraction evident in his tone. "Medical examiner can compare the teeth in the photograph to the actual teeth."

"They don't need dental records? I always thought they needed dental records to identify bodies."

"If you have them, they're great, but as you heard, we don't have any dental records this time."

"Oh. And also, you told Mrs. Odam she could identify the body using photographs. Doesn't she have to go into the morgue? You know, that scene on television where they slide the body out of the refrigerator and whip back the sheet, revealing the grotesque remains?"

Muñoz turned back to me and I got a slow stare. The deputy enjoyed a chuckle. "That's not really how it happens," Muñoz said. We'll take the Odams, or whoever they are, into an interview room and show them photographs of the boy's face.

72

If there are any identifying marks on the body, we'll have pictures of those, too."

"Our photographer's a whiz," the deputy contributed. "She can almost make the face look alive, like the guy's asleep."

Muñoz grunted. "I can already tell you though, whoever he is, the kid in the picture Mrs. Odam gave me is the same guy as the body in our morgue." He looked out the window, staring grimly at one lone steer standing under an oak as we passed. We approached the bottom of the grade.

"So the body is almost certainly their son, Chip." I stated this as a matter of fact, since all the evidence pointed that way. "And if that's true, how did he die? Someone must have murdered him. And how likely is it that parents would kill their own son? So even though the FBI thinks these people are bad guys, they wouldn't have any direct connection with the death you're investigating. I mean, other than being the parents. Right?"

"Making a lot of assumptions again," he said. He glanced over his shoulder one more time at me, then did a double-take through the rear window.

"Get down," he growled, his right hand going for the gun under his jacket. I only looked long enough to see the black car behind us racing up on our tail. If a less risk-averse person was telling this story, they could have described what happened next. Me, I hit the floor boards and stayed there, well out of the way in case bullets started flying.

"Oh, geez!" I heard Muñoz say, then a long squeal from behind us. Our SUV wavered slightly but kept rolling.

"You want me to stop?" the deputy said.

That's when I popped up, just in time to see the black FBI car take the first exit at the bottom of the grade going way too fast. It went briefly airborne, then all we saw was a cloud of dust. There was no sign of the Odam's car.

"You want me to find that other car, give chase?" the deputy said, excited.

"No. Take this next exit and go back around. We should give aid to the agents in that car," Muñoz said. "We've lost the Odams, probably for good."

After we'd made sure the two FBI agents had survived their fender-bender with the guard rail bordering the exit lane with only bruised egos, Muñoz suggested that, since we were so close, we should go on to the office of the medical examiner.

I had misgivings. I did recall that at the time I had accepted the sheriff's offer of a consulting contract, I asked for assurance that I would never have to attend autopsies or spend time staring at dead bodies. Heaven knows, there's already enough of that on television. My contract was merely a formality so the county's insurance company wouldn't pitch a fit about me riding around in the sheriff's vehicles. Even then, until that day I had only ridden in Detective Muñoz's unmarked sedan. And here I was, not only riding in a big white SUV with the sheriff's decal on the door and the word "sheriff" painted in big green letters across the back, but I was sitting in the back seat behind the grill like some low-life criminal. And now he wanted me to go to the medical examiner's office with him and look at a body? I started to squawk, but by then we were already pulling into the parking lot of a low, nondescript building not far from the hospital.

Muñoz let me out, since of course, the door handles on the inside had been rendered inoperable, cutting down on the number of criminal passengers making unauthorized exits. Inside, I did not find steel tables, instruments of torture, or drains in the floor. Instead, Muñoz led me to a small conference room furnished almost like someone's tastefully decorated living room, complete with subdued lighting.

"Is this where the families identify bodies?" I said, looking around for a way for corpses to be wheeled in.

"Yeah, well, photographs actually. Again, we almost never have to ask families to look at the actual body." He left, and returned after a few minutes with a cold can of soda and a woman in a white coat, her hair covered in a coral-colored hijab. Her badge identified her as Nazanin Rajavi, forensic pathologist. Muñoz asked her to join us at the table, and we began to pepper her with questions. She had no more answers than before. She promised autopsy results by the next morning, providing there were no additional interruptions. We all expressed our disappointment that the Odam's had chosen not to join us and identify their son.

With gratitude, I accepted Muñoz's offer of a ride home in his official, yet unmarked, sedan. From her front porch, Freda gave me a big suggestive wink as we passed. One day I would need to explain to her why Muñoz and I were never going to be the romantic item she continually hinted about, but this was not that day. I waved gaily and let her think whatever she wished.

I settled myself on the porch, this time with my novel and a plate of semi-homemade cookies, those kind where all you do is slice and bake them. That was enough law enforcement consultation for the time being. I was just getting serious about reading when I realized it was time to head over to the sheep ranch. Bagging the cookies to go, I loaded the dogs into our rental and grabbed a notebook to jot down critical notes for the herding of Inez's sheep.

My dog Shiner, one of Inez's dogs, and I would be responsible for bringing in the flock in for the night for three days while Inez and her most accomplished border collie went off to compete in the Soldier Hollow Sheepdog Championship in Utah.

What with all the excitement, it was close to four o'clock by the time we pulled up to the ranch gate and let ourselves inside.

Scout is eager, but really too old to help much with the stock, so I secured him inside his usual day-care kennel where he promptly fell asleep on the grass in the sun. Inez handed me a fiberglass pole about four feet long, and pointed us toward the gate at the end of the arena to try our luck without her to guide us.

I had been looking forward to meandering around the golden hills with a crook like the one pictured in that painting of Jesus on velvet at my cousin Carla's house, but the fiberglass pole turned out to be the only tool provided. And a single command, "get around" sent Shiner and Inez's dog on their outrun over the hills to gather and bring in the sheep. They quickly disappeared over the closest knoll. I stood there feeling sort of useless.

While I waited for the dogs to return with the sheep, I tried to entertain myself by twirling the pole like a baton. It whirled impressively for a turn or two, then inexplicably flew to the side, nearly clipping a seagull who had settled on the grass nearby. The seagull wisely took flight just as a group of about a dozen sheep trotted into sight to my left. The dogs were supposed to find and bring in forty-five sheep. I wondered what I would do if they came back with forty-four sheep. After a couple of dozen sheep had hustled into view, I began to be concerned about how I would get an accurate count. They all looked sort of alike, and constantly milled about, peering over their shoulders for the rest of the herd and those menacing dogs.

Crouching low as they ran, both dogs appeared and pushed more sheep toward the gate. Lucky for me, Inez joined me as they drew closer.

"How am I going to know if they're all here?" I asked. Inez dug a hand-held plastic counter out of her bag and showed me how to click it each time a sheep went through the gate.

I swung the gate wide enough to let in two or three ewes at a time, and tried to count as I clicked, but really, forty-five, forty-four? Who could tell? The dogs seemed convinced they hadn't left anyone behind, and that was good enough for me. The clicker said forty-three. Anxiously, I turned to find Inez just finishing her own count.

"Forty-five," she said. "The dogs will let you know if they've had to leave anyone out there. Just watch their behavior. You can always get one of the guys to help you saddle up so you can go look, if you think someone's gone lame and been left behind, but one of the dogs will stay with a lame ewe. You'll never find one ewe without the dogs." This was probably not the time to tell Inez I had not been on the back of a horse since that one time in Brownie Scouts.

We strolled back toward the barn where we made sure the stock tanks were filled with fresh water. The two Pyrennes dogs were already roving among the flock. Those dogs would protect the sheep while they rested inside the arena. Promising again that we would be there in the evenings to bring in the flock, my dogs and I headed for home.

CHAPTER NINE

The sound of a car pulling into the driveway awakened me Thursday morning. As long as I live, I'll never understand these people who not only awaken before dawn, but are also able to shower, shave, and show up at your door before the sun clears the horizon, and dressed to the nines. A musky aftershave wafted my way.

Of course, in the canyon they way we are, the sun takes its own sweet time climbing to the horizon, so it wasn't really all that early. Still, not one ray had yet peeped over the hills when Muñoz tapped on my kitchen door. He lifted a pastry bag by way of greeting. For my part, I was attired in my bathrobe, bedroom slippers, and lucky Giants baseball cap. I can smell a cheese danish at ten feet, and hurriedly started the coffee.

"Also got the autopsy results," he said, sliding a paper from an inside pocket.

"Hmm. Cheese danish, a good cup of coffee, and an autopsy report. Maybe we could look at that after the danish?"

"Makes no difference to me. Mostly, it adds to the confusion."

I took a warm, sweet bite and chewed, knowing something gruesome was soon to follow.

"Pathologist found enough alcohol and rohypnol—they call those roofies—in the boy's blood to render a person that size unconscious for a good long time. Says ..." and he referred to the paper. "possibly even enough to bring him close to death, especially since the guy also had alcohol in his system. Very little alcohol. Barely measurable. There were no other signs of trauma." Muñoz pointed at one line. "Called the manner of death 'suspicious slash unknown.' She wasn't willing to make a final call yet."

"No trauma, huh? Is she suggesting the boy drugged himself? So, suicide?"

"No way to know without more investigation. That's where you come in. We need to find a way to determine his state of mind at the time of death. With the water in his lungs, he might even have tried to drown himself."

"You mean like, he took a bunch of roofies and threw himself in the ocean, wrapped in a sheet and tied with dock line?"

"Unlikely, huh? Dr. Rajavi says not enough roofies to kill him, and not enough water in the lungs to drown."

"Maybe he under-estimated how much of the drug to take. Then, when he jumped in the water, he came to, and couldn't go through with it."

"Possibly." Muñoz was staring, waiting for me to think the thing through. Waiting for the light to go on. I'd had at least another three sips of the strong coffee before it hit me.

"Even if all that happened, he failed and didn't die ... but now he's dead. So either he made another, more successful attempt, or someone else came along and finished him off."

"The dead part is right. Guy is definitely dead."

"And regardless of how he died, someone went to some length to dispose of his body. All by itself, that part is mysterious."

"Yeah. He didn't wrap himself up in that sheet."

I thought about that. How the body arrived on the beach bundled like that was a puzzle we didn't yet have enough pieces to put together. We needed to find out more about Chip, his life, his family, and his friends. "So where do you suggest we start? Can we try to talk to his parents again, or maybe his sister?"

"We could, except, remember? We lost the Odams."

"You can't even find the car?"

"Nope."

"Uh-oh, hang on."

"What?"

"Just hang on a minute." I dashed back to the bedroom, rummaged in the dirty clothes hamper, and came up with Tuesday's shorts. Thank heavens, the piece of paper with the license number was still tucked in the watch pocket. I carried it out and handed it to the detective.

"What's this?"

"It's the license number from the black car up at the big house." I tried to imbue my tone with enough impatience so he wouldn't ask me why I hadn't given him this number before. If he got the idea I was incompetent, I risked losing my consultant-to-the-sheriff status.

He pulled his notebook out, flipped through a few pages, then stopped and read, comparing a notation to the number I had given him. "Different number," he said. "The car the Odam's were in yesterday is registered to a rental agency, and rented to the same property management company handling the house. I'll have to check this one."

"So there's more than one car up there."

He grunted in a vaguely affirmative manner while copying the number into his notebook.

"Also," I said, "we saw two mobster-like guys in the car Tuesday morning, but on Wednesday only one mobster drove the Odams, so maybe there's another mobster left up in the house?"

"Watching the girl, possibly."

"They're really gone? The parents just took off yesterday and they're not coming back?"

"Appears so. They never came back here, and, like I said, we've been unable to locate them or their car."

"Hmm. If they're hiding from the FBI, too, we might never see hide nor hair of them again."

"Could be." Muñoz polished of the last of his danish and carefully wiped his fingers. "I'm heading up to the house now. See if anyone is left there. Want to come?"

I declined, pointing out that I was still attired in my fluffy bathrobe. I did suggest he stop back by if he learned anything new.

Curiously, black cars with tinted windows were still cruising the canyon that morning, at least twice. Maybe FBI, maybe someone else. What we needed was some kind of more comprehensive surveillance. I considered the possibility of sneaking up the trail behind the house and spying at the back from behind a bush. Then I thought about those boar. Or possibly a rattlesnake. Or even a confrontation with that other mobster. Wondered when I had gotten to be such a wuss.

I walked up to the house Bryce shares with his parents and, after the obligatory conversation about how poorly they all were doing, I was able to persuade Bryce to fly his drone over the yard surrounding the big house. We had to set up on Amanita's porch to have a clear path to launch, and Bryce's father, Ernie, insisted on being wheeled along, so we had a bit of an audience. Bryce proved to be better skilled at getting the drone to hold still while peering through a window than I had any reason to expect. We could tell someone was moving inside, but we didn't see Mr. or Mrs. Odam, or even Sissy.

I called Muñoz to report about our limited success with Bryce's drone, and he got all excited. Apparently, the sheriff's department had recently acquired its own drone for exactly this type of surveillance. He went off to find the technical guy who was learning to fly the drone while I sat on hold wondering how I felt about law enforcement drones peering into my yard and through my windows. I suppose I could have worked up a bit more righteous indignation if I was the sort of person who ever engaged in any activity that law enforcement might find of interest.

Muñoz finally returned to the phone and said he and the technical guy would be right out with their drone. Theirs had a more sophisticated camera. It also had a longer battery life, so the technician would be able to make his drone lurk outside the house much longer.

Muñoz, the technician, and I parked ourselves on Amanita's porch. This time, she wasn't home and Ernie was absorbed in his afternoon nap, so we had a little more privacy. The three of us settled in front of the laptop to watch as the drone began its journey up to and around the big house.

There wasn't much going on for a while, although we thought we saw movement inside.

"Hey, look, there," the technician pointed. "That door is opening."

Sure enough, a door in the back opened and the large dog emerged. Assuming the dog had not opened the door, at least one person still had to be in the house. The dog wandered for few minutes, sniffing the air and inspecting the fence line.

"Looks like he's trying to find a way out," Muñoz said.

"Maybe just checking wildlife activity," I suggested, always the dog expert.

"Here comes someone else."

We watched as a young man matching the description Freda had given of the passenger in the black car stepped out, probably keeping an eye on the dog.

"What's that guy doing?" The technician leaned over, peering at the screen in excitement. "He's putting something wrapped in plastic under that bush, see that? Is he planting some kind of a device under there?"

"What, like a land mine?" Muñoz said. "Or a web cam?"

"Something like that."

Muñoz cut me a glance, a twinkle in his eye. As the recent adopter of a young puppy, Muñoz knew exactly what the guy was doing with the plastic bag. I decided to let him be the dog expert this time.

"I suspect he's picking up dog poop," Muñoz said, as we watched the guy tie off the first bag and pull a second over his hand. "A stunningly large pile of dog poop."

Nobody is an expert yet at flying those drones. The technician squinted at the control console as he steered, trying to maneuver the device to get a good face shot of the guy in the yard.

"Uh-oh," I said, a moment too late. The drone had gotten too close. When the guy stood, he saw the device just over his head. We watched as he calmly pulled an ugly handgun out of a shoulder holster previously hidden under his jacket, aimed, and blew the drone right out of the air. The screen went black.

"Oh, brother," I groaned, while Muñoz slammed one fist on his thigh. The technician only stared at the screen in disbelief.

"Sheriff's not going to be happy about that," he said.

Whether we'd been watching too many crime programs on television, or with mobsters in the neighborhood we'd been expecting it, neither Nina nor I were too surprised to hear what sounded like a shotgun blast, and then a second, as we were having a peaceful candlelit meal on her front porch that evening. Shiner jumped the steps from the yard to the porch in a single leap and cowered at my feet before the second shot echoed through the canyon. Scout lifted his head from his paws, but his hearing is going, so he displayed no undue alarm.

"*Dios mio,*" Nina said. "What now?" We heard some angry yelling, had to be Bryce, then two more blasts.

This is a rural neighborhood, and is often populated with unexpected visitors of both human and non-human species. Generally though, we don't go around shooting at one another, despite our many differences. I decided there was no sense in getting worked up, at least until dinner was finished. I forked up another bite of *crepas con huevos,* and chewed while awaiting the next development.

We didn't have long to wait. Headlights cruised slowly down Arroyo Loco Road, and Grant's 1990s Buick LeSabre rolled up. Helen leaned out the window.

"Hey! You guys see those boar go by?"

Oh, brother. Apparently Arroyo Loco's local pack of wild boar were making another visit. I've heard they can be dangerous, but so far our pack had never exceeded the bounds of conventional propriety. I was more concerned about injuries caused by randomly flying shotgun pellets than potential boar attacks.

I glanced at Nina, and she at me. In almost the same breath, we said, "They went that way!" and pointed out to the relatively unpopulated highway. Helen looked skeptical, but

84

she directed Grant forward, and the car rolled out of sight in that direction. A few moments later, Bryce padded downhill and stopped at Nina's. He was wearing his bedroom slippers and carrying a baseball bat.

"Did you see the boars?" he said, panting as he climbed up and plopped himself down on a step. "Helen said they were rooting in Lauren's flower bed again."

I helped myself to an authentic homemade Mexican chocolate chip cookie and considered my answer. Although they can be a nuisance, and dangerous if cornered, the wild boar are as native to this region as are humans. Rooting in flower beds hardly seems like a capital offense, punishable by bludgeoning with a baseball bat. Nina's thoughts were running along the same lines.

"Were you planning to beat them to death, Bryce?"

He turned the bat in his hands, while I contemplated that scenario.

"Um, no, of course not. I just thought, well, I should have something to defend myself with, you know, if they attacked me."

I weighed my words. "If you're concerned about being attacked by wild boar, Bryce, wouldn't it be better to stay inside your house instead of running around out here in the dark? Especially in, what are those, your bedroom slippers?" I could tell I'd gone one step too far when his jaw tightened.

"And how are you getting home tonight, Estela?" he said. "You and your dogs. Your car is up in your driveway. Are you planning on walking home alone in the dark?"

This gave me pause. I hated to admit it, but Bryce had a point. Maybe I should ask him and his trusty baseball bat to escort the dogs and me. This plan was dashed when, next door Raymond tottered out onto his porch and squinted into the darkness, no doubt searching for the source of the earlier noise. Bryce rose, launched himself across to Raymond's porch and settled in for a good long chat. Guess Bryce wasn't going to walk me home any time soon.

Raymond cast an accusing glance in our direction, as though Nina and I might have had something to do with the gunfire. She shrugged and I continued innocently munching on cookies. Grant and Helen cruised past again, heading home a few moments later. I probably would have found that more reassuring if Nina and I had not fibbed about seeing the boar running toward the highway. As it was, we had no idea where the animals might be lurking. In the end, I gave Nina a choice between driving the dogs and me home or putting the three of us up for the night, and she got out the keys to her brand new Lexus. I couldn't remember the last time I'd brushed the loose fur off the dogs, but I guess that's why car-sized vacuum cleaners were invented.

The phone jangled me from under the covers Friday morning. If Muñoz kept this up, I'd be able to toss my alarm clock. I grumbled a sleepy hello.

"Got some more results here," he said, with no preamble.

I kind of miss the days when the phone did not display the incoming caller's name, and everyone had to announce themselves and inquire into my health before launching into the latest update.

"Wanted to get your thoughts on this," he continued.

"Okay, shoot." There was a brief sound that might have been a single chuckle. I guess inviting a law enforcement officer to shoot might be found amusing, although that had not been my intent.

"Dr. Rajavi says the body shows signs of having been tied around the legs with weights. Bruises and so on."

"Hmm. That makes sense, right? If you're going to dump a corpse into a body of water, you'd want to weigh it down somehow. You know, so it wouldn't float and wash ashore. Oh, except this one did wash ashore."

"Yeah, she thinks the weight fell off."

"Fell off?"

"Yeah. You know, it wasn't on the body when we found it."

"It came untied or something? That seems kind of amateurish. Does that mean the murder was committed by someone who didn't know much about disposing properly of murder victims?"

"Pathologist says her best guess is the body was weighted, then the weight slid partially off, letting the body float just above the ocean floor until the movement of waves and the tide tore it loose and it washed ashore with the rest of that junk."

"Yuck. Kind of early for the gruesome details, don't you think?"

"Huh?"

"Never mind. It still seems to me like a professional, like a mobster, would know better how to get rid of a body. I mean, even dumping it right off shore like that seems like something a rookie would do. Wouldn't the waves eventually bring in pieces as the body started to decompose?" I didn't really hear what I was saying until the words were out of my mouth. I gulped. "I just mean ..."

"Yeah, yeah, I know what you mean."

"So, is she willing to make a call yet on the cause of death?"

"Nope. Highly suspicious. Between our visit though, and the confusion about the identity, I think this case has got her curious. She's still looking." We agreed that piquing the pathologist's curiosity in such a confusing case had to be a positive thing.

This seemed like as good a time as any to give the dogs a run on the beach. Almost a week had passed, so surely all signs of the body would have been removed. The tide may have even taken away the pile of debris that washed ashore with the sad bundle.

Besides, I had been practicing my birding skills at home, and had some questions for a more experienced hobbyist like Evan. I parked in my usual spot near the hole in the fence, looped Papa's recently exhumed binoculars around my neck, and started the trek north along the shore. The tide was out, giving me hard beach sand at the water's edge on which to walk. The dogs raced ahead, enjoying our faster-than-usual pace.

We saw no signs of Jax on the beach, but as we approached Evan's small home, the retriever loped out to greet us. Evan himself sat in one of the weathered chairs, peering in my direction through his binoculars. Guess he'd seen me coming. I waved and he set his binoculars on the arm of the chair and gestured for me to join him. The dogs were allowed to continue to romp in the sand, close enough to stay in sight.

After the usual greetings, I launched into my first question.

"So, Evan, the other day I was using these binoculars to look at a bird on the fence at my house. A little bird. She kept chirping and I could swear she was chirping right at me. And I noticed she was black and white. I've always thought those little birds were all gray or brownish, but when I looked through the binoculars, she was definitely black and white. You know, with a kind of a black cape over her head, and then around her shoulders? Every so often, it looked like she had a black hat with a pointy tip. Do you know what that bird was? I called her a dusky flycatcher, but do you know what she was, really?"

"Did you look it up?"

"You mean like in a bird book?"

He smiled and tipped his head, like you might at a particularly obtuse child.

"Well, no. I couldn't find my dad's book. Anyway, it would be kind of old, so maybe out of date?"

"Old bird books are usually okay. Bird feather fashions don't change that much, year-to-year. Sometimes people change what they call the birds. Sharp-shinned hawks used to be sparrow hawks, and bird ranges change over time. But the birds still look the same. The bird you're describing sounds like a phoebe, and probably a male if the cape was dark and distinctive."

"Phoebe, huh? She ... he flew off the fence every once in a while, did a sort of a little jig in mid-air, and went back to the fence."

"Yep, that's a flycatcher, which phoebes are. He wasn't doing a jig. Every time he flew out like that he was catching a tiny bug. If you had better quality binoculars, you might have been able to see the bug."

I knew sooner or later someone was going to remark on my antique binoculars. "Yes, okay. I should get new ones, huh? Maybe next time I'm in the bird food store."

He was nodding again. "And it wouldn't hurt to pick up a field guide so you can identify what you're seeing, and get up-to-date information on ranges."

I furrowed my brow at him and he explained more.

"The range of many bird species are moving northward as the climate changes. And the range maps are good for narrowing down your identifications. For example, you saw this bird at your house in June. That means it was probably a black phoebe. If this was December, it might just as easily have been a Say's phoebe. A good field guide will help you make those finer distinctions. See, here's the black phoebe." He held his book open just like my kindergarten teacher used to do, and just like a child, I gazed intently at the picture. I like learning new information, but all of this detail made my brain feel full.

"What did you do for a living, Evan? You sure know a lot about this stuff." My first guess was that he was too young to be retired. On the other hand, here he was, home again in the middle of a week day. In fact, he was almost always on the beach when I stopped by with my dogs. I didn't see where he would have time to work, unless he worked at home. I didn't get an answer. I made eye contact. He glanced away. Apparently he was reluctant to talk about his job. I hadn't meant to be intrusive, but his response made me curious. I waited.

"I teach biology," he finally said, "at the high school."

CHAPTER TEN

I digested the information that Evan taught biology at the high school. That would explain why he was almost always on the beach at the same time I was there. We had similar work schedules.

"I'm on summer break," he said.

Teaching at the high school might also mean he had known Chip. "That body you and I found," I turned to look that direction. "Muñoz says he was a high school kid."

"Sort of," Evan said.

"Sort of?" I turned back to Evan and tried to gentle my voice. "Did you know him."

Evan paused before replying. "I knew of him. Chip and his so-called sister. They weren't there very long. Not more than a few weeks. Odd situation, but we could never figure out just what. But not good. No, I didn't really know either of them, and now it seems they've quit coming to school anyway. You should talk to the some of the other kids."

"Hmm," I said. "Good idea."

I peered out across the gentle ocean with Evan's superior binoculars. "I don't suppose you saw the body, or that pile of debris floating in on the tide the other morning. I mean, do you have any idea where it came from? Muñoz and I think it could have been dumped off a boat somewhere off shore, but not too far away." I might have been overstating our conclusion. On the other hand, we had to eliminate some of the possibilities or we'd never figure this thing out. I took the glasses from my eyes and stared back at Evan.

He shook his head. "High tide was around five in the morning that day. Even if I'd been up, it would have been too dark to see anything."

"Hmm." This was discouraging.

"I can tell you one thing, though. That pile landed about there." He pointed south along the beach. "Which means it came from out there." Here, he pointed slightly north and out to sea.

"How do you know that?"

"Because there's a current all along here. It flows north to south along the coast. Anything that washes up during a high tide comes from somewhere north of here."

This could be extremely useful information, although I wasn't quite sure where it fit into the picture we were building.

"So, if the body was dumped off a boat, the boat would have been up there, north of here?"

"Most likely."

"Is there any way to know where it would be now?"

"You mean, if the boat floated in on its own? Because more likely someone would have motored or rowed it, meaning it could be anywhere."

"Muñoz says the medical examiner says the body was weighted when it was originally dumped."

"What, you mean like with cement overshoes?"

"Oh, yes, that's how its supposed to be done isn't it? No, this guy just had a weight of some kind tied around his ankles with that blue rope. The weight fell off."

'Doesn't sound like whoever disposed of that body knew much about what they were doing." He gazed pensively out across the blue-gray waves.

"That was my conclusion, too."

My cell phone rang just as I was finishing off a couple of tasty fish tacos at Pacitos *taqueria*. The FBI agent, Roybal, wanted to meet with Muñoz and me at my house in an hour to share information.

I had just enough time to swing by the wild bird store and pick up a lightweight pair of binoculars equipped with the latest in focusing technology. I also purchased the newest edition of the field guide Evan had recommended, a large sack of oil sunflower seed, and a pricey squirrel-proof feeder. I filled the rest of my shopping bag with fliers and brochures about up-coming birding festivals and outdoor excursions. As I drove the winding highway home, I tried to calculate how sizable a check I might expect from the sheriff when this investigation wrapped up, hoping the funds would be sufficient to cover this unexpectedly expensive new birding hobby.

The FBI agents in the car that flew off the grade road in pursuit of the Odams had suffered only minor injuries, although due to something major with the suspension, their car was a total loss. The replacement black sedan made a trip past my house that afternoon, a single agent at the wheel. Presumably he was still trying to roust out the occupants of the big house. Still without probable cause, and so still without a warrant, the agent did not have any better luck than previously. By the time his black car reappeared on the road in front, Muñoz had arrived. We settled on the porch for our meeting.

Young and freshly-shaven, Agent Roybal seemed anxious to solicit our help in identifying the couple living in the big house.

For our part, we wanted to identify the boy found dead on the beach.

"As you know," Roybal started, "We're looking for a guy, a criminal, who escaped our net, and we think this Odam living up here might be our guy."

"So, who is this Mr. Odam? Somebody really dangerous?" I asked.

"To be honest," Roybal continued, "we're not sure how violent or dangerous he might be, but we suspect very. If this is our guy, we collared him last year and got him to accept a plea deal. He works for all kinds of bad guys, gangsters, organized crime. Even foreign governments. He's a skilled counterfeiter, known for producing untraceable false identification papers of all kinds."

"You had him locked up?" Muñoz said.

"We did have him in protective custody. Not exactly locked up, because he had not been convicted of anything ... yet. He had agreed to testify in federal court in a case that would have put a couple of serious mobsters behind bars for good, and possibly opened up some issues having to do with national security. Classified." He gave each of us a long stare, as though we might not otherwise comprehend the gravity of the situation. "He'd given us valuable information about the convert operations of at least one unfriendly foreign power. So we had him in a safe house with two agents."

"And he got away?" Muñoz said.

"More like he was sprung by the mobsters, or someone. Several guys raided the house early one morning and more-or-less kidnapped him. Both agents were shot. Both survived. Malakov was set to testify, then he was set to enter witness protection.

"Who?" I said.

"Malakov. Alexei Malakov. That's our guy."

"So his real name isn't Yaxshi Odam?" Muñoz asked.

"Or Bravo Ragazzo?" I echoed.

Roybal furrowed his brow, looking confused. "My Uzbeck is rusty," he said, "but I think 'yaxshi odam' means something like good guy."

Muñoz raised his eyebrows. We probably shouldn't have been so surprised. Turned out those mobster guys really had been yanking our chain.

"Okay, never mind," I said. "Alexei Malakov. Okay. Sorry I interrupted. Please, go on."

"So, he and his family were going into witness protection?" Muñoz said. "The son and daughter, too?"

"Sorry, I don't know. You're the one who told me there's a family involved. We just had Malakov. I never heard anything about a family before you said something."

"Not even his wife?" I said.

Roybal shook his head. "Not that we heard about. In fact, once we heard there was a whole family living here, we backed off. Assumed this Odam guy wasn't Malakov."

"And now you're sure the guy living in the big house is Malakov?" I said.

"Yes. After some additional research, including the testimony of a former associate of Malakov's we're certain that's our guy. And now he's disappeared again. Spooked."

Sounded like there was note of blame in Agent Roybal's voice. After all, if Muñoz hadn't insisted those people follow him to identify the body, they might still be holed up in the big house.

"Huh." Muñoz said. "Who the blazes is this body we've got then, if it's not the son of the couple living up there?"

We studied Roybal's face. He spread his palms over his shoulders. "Wish I could help you, but we really don't know. Could be just some random bad guy who crossed the wrong mobster. You're waiting on DNA?"

Muñoz nodded.

"That could take a while, I know. I can tell you the body is almost certainly the young guy who was living in this house up the hill, and who was attending the high school under the name Chip Odam. We have evidence linking the two, including fingerprints, photo id, and eyewitness testimony. So we know that much. His prints don't show up in the National Crime Information Center, or any other data base. Without a name, it's hard to do a complete search. Beyond that, we really have no idea as to his identity. I'll sure let you know if we learn anything as part of our investigation. In the meantime, we need to track down this Malakov character."

"I have a question," I said. "How come the mobsters didn't just kill Malakov so he couldn't testify against them?" I almost added something about how that's what always happens in the movies, but wisely, I did not.

"Malakov is more valuable to the mob alive. He's a gifted counterfeiter and forger of documents, plus he's brilliant at coming up with lucrative scams. We think the reason the mob sprang him was because he accepted a better offer from them. They could put him under their protection, which is what we think is happening up at that house. Now the mob can continue to use his skills for their own ends. But, as you know, he's gone again," Roybal said, his shoulders drooping.

"Any chance the FBI investigation could get us into the house?" Muñoz said. "Might even be something in there that would tell us where they've gone."

There was a long silence while we thought through the possibilities.

"Some goon who's there now just shot the sheriff's brand new drone all to hell," Muñoz offered. "Would that give us grounds for a search warrant?"

Roybal considered the question. "The residents on the lease are missing, and someone not on the lease is occupying the house and firing weapons? We might be able to get a search warrant with that."

"Or I could do a wellness-check," Muñoz said. "We think the girl, Sissy, might still be there."

I gave him my worried-mother look. "Yes, if you are in the mood to get shot, too."

"There's that." Roybal said. He stood and shook out the sharp creases over the knees of his slacks. "Going up there now does't sound like the best idea. Why don't you let me get on the search warrant thing, and possibly I can get a SWAT team down here. The Malakovs left the house in a hurry, so possibly they did leave something useful behind.

I didn't feel like thinking about crime or fugitives or dead bodies any more that day. At long last I had time to make an inroad on that novel I wanted to get read. I curled up on the porch swing and promptly drifted off to sleep. A morning in the sea air often has that effect on me. My nap lasted until close to dinner time.

I was just starting to wonder what I could pull together for my evening meal when my phone rang with a much better offer from Muñoz. It seemed the FBI had learned that a boat currently docked at the marina near the state park in Morro Bay was registered to a Yaxshi Odam. Muñoz was on his way to take a look at the boat, and invited me to join him for dinner at the Bayside Marina, one of our favorite spots.

I thought it was suspiciously lucky to discover this boat belonging to the very people we were looking for, but it turns out that while people and guns can readily change identities and disappear, boats and cars have to carry their identification every place they go, and be registered and display their licenses at all times. The FBI investigators had located the boat through its state registration.

As we devoured our shared bowl of steamers, we discussed the possibility that the boat in question may have transported the body out to sea. Although we had no search warrant, we could still look at the boat from the pier on which it was moored. The sun was nearing the western horizon and shadows were long when we got a good look at it.

Being one of the largest vessels at the marina, the thirty-five foot cabin cruiser in question was moored at the deepest end of the lagoon, nearest the locked entrance to the pier. We both spent several minutes examining the boat through the gate, but saw nothing usual or even of interest. Beside the cabin door we could make out a tipped over waste bin spilling out several empty beer cans. A single damp-looking beach towel was draped over one of the outside benches. Whoever had cleaned the boat after its last outing had done a decidedly lackadaisical job, but nothing that might be considered evidence was visible from our perspective. We listened to the creaking of other boats and lines shifting in the out-going tide. Seagulls called from above.

"So much for that," Muñoz said. "Another dead end."

"So to speak," I added, thinking about the body on the beach.

Muñoz didn't even crack a smile. "I think I've got enough to get a warrant, get an evidence unit out here, at least dust for prints."

"Those darn warrants." I was still staring at the boat. Something was missing. I wasn't seeing anything so much as I was seeing a vacant space. Then I noticed the empty clamp at the back. Again, I thought, it's not what I'm seeing, it's what I'm not seeing.

"What goes there?" I said, pointing.

"Where?"

"There. You see? There's a device, looks like to clamp something down, but nothing's there. And another one on the other side."

Muñoz narrowed his eyes at the place I pointed. "That's got to be where a skiff or dinghy goes."

"A skiff?"

"Yeah, you know, like a small boat."

"A life raft?"

"Sort of, yeah. Or a dinghy. A boat this size would have a smaller boat on board."

"Well, there's nothing there now."

"Nope. Guess we'd better find out what happened to that. Possibly get the newspaper to run something. See if anyone knows where it went."

"Yes, good idea." A name scripted across the back in black paint caught my attention. "Poddelka. That's an odd name. Do you know what it means?"

He crinkled his brow and shrugged.

"Sounds like one of those pastries Freda brings to potlucks." Something else nagged at me. I scanned the boat again, slowly, from the bow to the stern, and then back.

"What?"

"I'm not sure. There's something here, though … " I zeroed in on the waste bin. "This would make an amazing party boat. I mean, if you were into that sort of activity."

"You think someone had a party here?"

"Well, I know it doesn't look much like it now, but the medical examiner did say the boy had roofies in his system, right? Isn't that a party drug?"

"Kind of a leap from that to this boat."

"I know. Still. Maybe a waiter up at the restaurant. Someone might know if there have been parties here."

Muñoz shrugged. "Let's go ask."

At first we had no luck finding anyone who had seen any parties on that boat. The other waiters pointed us to Roberto, the head waiter and maitre d'. Roberto worked most weekend evenings, and was also responsible for arranging restaurant deliveries to boats moored at the marina. It turned out he was quite familiar with the Odam's cabin-cruiser, the numerous parties hosted on board, and Chip Odam in particular.

"Rude and obnoxious" was Roberto's summation of Chip's personality. "Plus, he's a lousy tipper, even when we hand deliver food onboard. And I personally suspect that many of the young people at those parties are underage. Plus, he has girls there. And drugs. In my opinion."

Roberto, who insisted we call him "Bob," which didn't sound very waiterly to me, was warming to his topic.

"What about the parents?" Muñoz said. "Are they ever here? Do they know about these parties?"

"Oh, well, Mr. and Mrs. Odam are very nice people. Very nice. Mr. Odam, he's quite generous. He always offers me a drink when I deliver food to the Poddelka. But, no, no, I don't think they do know about the young people's parties. In fact …." Roberto seemed to consider his words for a moment.

100

"One night, last week I think it was, I had to call them. There had been another party there, not noisy, but a few young people. Then it was quiet, and I thought everyone had left. We were getting ready to close up here. I looked out that way, and I saw Chip kind of standing. Well, he was stumbling around, you know, drunk."

I glanced back toward the boat, but even with lights on the pier it was not that easy to make out details. "How did you know it was Chip?" I asked.

"Oh, because I had to fish him out. One minute he was standing there, kind of leaning, and the next, I heard a splash. I figured, you know, he'd fallen in. So I went out there. We have a key to the gate because we have to deliver to the boats all along the pier there, and so I went out there and there he was, splashing around in the water. Fell off the boat."

"Was he swimming?" Muñoz asked.

"Thrashing, but not even that, much. I hauled him onto the pier by his collar. Drunk, I guess. He wanted to pass out right there. I helped him back onto the boat. Told him to go inside and sleep it off."

"And he was drunk, but alive when you left him?"

"Good heavens, man! What do you mean? Of course he was alive!"

Muñoz and I glanced at each other, then looked away.

"Well, actually," I said, "Chip has left us." Muñoz gave me a quizzical look. My words were awkward, I know. On the other hand, this was my first time delivering the bad news, and I didn't know Roberto ... Bob. He stared at me in horror, so I assumed he'd gotten the point.

"Dead?" he said.

"Yes, I'm afraid so."

"On the Poddelka? This was more than a week ago. You're just finding him now?"

I let Muñoz explain the details, and reassure Bob that he was under no suspicion. Muñoz asked him if he knew anything more.

"Oh, I know it was none of my business," Bob said, "but Mr. Odam has always been so nice. I called him to tell him about Chip. I thought it was only right that the parents should know their kid was out here."

"You called the parents and told them Chip was on their boat, drunk?" Muñoz clarified. We looked at each other again. I was wondering how the parents had responded to that news.

"Yup, I did," Bob said.

Muñoz jotted down something in his notebook. "And who did you speak to when you called? This was late at night, correct? Who answered the phone?"

"Yup. About eleven. We were closing up. And I didn't actually talk to anyone. They had the answering machine on, so I left a message. That made me a little nervous. I mean, what if Chip got home and heard my message? I just felt I had to do something."

"You did the right thing." Muñoz assured him with an earnest look. "And then what happened? Did the parents come to get Chip?"

"Oh, we all left. It was closing time and I went home, along with everyone else."

"So you don't know if anyone came to get Chip?" Muñoz made a final dot in his notes and flipped the book closed, while Bob shook his head.

Muñoz thanked him and turned to go, but I had a couple more questions.

"You left a message on the answering machine at the Odam's house, and you have no way of knowing who listened to that message, or if anyone did?"

"No, ma'am."

Muñoz gave me a long blank look, as though he honestly had no idea where I was going with my question.

"So, Bob's message let someone at the house know where Chip was, that he was in bad shape, and possibly in need of help."

Muñoz nodded, waiting for me to make a point. Maybe I was making a leap too far. It just seemed to me like anyone could have responded to that message, and not necessarily with virtuous intent, given the crowd we were inquiring about.

We needed to know one more thing. There had apparently been numerous parties on that boat, and we didn't know the exact time, or even day, of Chip's death. In my view, we needed to pin the timeline down more tightly. After all, Bob hauling Chip out of the water might have had nothing to do with his death.

"Roberto ... "

"Bob," he said.

I gave him a thin smile. This had been a very long day. "We need to know what night this happened. Is there any way you can tell us what night Chip fell in the water?" Bob turned a distinctly uncooperative expression on me. I lifted my chin at Muñoz, who picked up the thread.

"Yeah, Bob. You saved Chip's life. You must remember which night that was. Did you write it down or anything?"

I was trying too hard not to roll my eyes to really hear Bob's answer. He saved Chip's life? So that someone else could kill him ten minutes later? When I tuned back in, Bob was flipping through the pages of his reservation book on the podium.

"Let's see here. I'm sure it was the same night we had that group from the university. Yup, here they are on Thursday at seven. So, yup, that had to be it. Thursday night."

As we backed out of our parking space, Muñoz said "Kind of surprised the Poddelka is even still here. When the Odams went missing ...."

"Malakovs."

"Uh-huh. Anyway, if they needed a way to disappear, why not take the boat?"

"Hmm. Maybe it's harder to disappear on a boat than in a car. Hey, hang on a second." I had spotted a familiar head in a dusty black sedan parked several spaces over. "Is that Roybal, you know, the FBI agent, parked there?"

"Could be. Looks like an unmarked. See the steelies?"

No idea what he was pointing at.

"Black wheels, no hubcaps. Good way to spot an unmarked."

"Okay, good to know. Anyway, what's Roybal doing here?"

"Probably thinking the same thing I was thinking. That someone might be coming for the Poddelka. He wants to be here when they get here."

That made sense, although sitting in a small sedan for days on end waiting didn't. There had to be an easier way.

"Oh," he said, "and I found out, Poddelka is a Russian word. It means counterfeit."

"Hmm. So not a pastry."

The detective only gave me a confused scowl.

CHAPTER ELEVEN

For a change of pace, the dogs and I were awakened at about five Saturday morning by a series of what had to be gun shots. Both dogs jumped on the bed with me. I rolled over to make room and we all settled down, ready to go back to sleep. Just before I drifted off, I hoped the boar had dodged the bullets, and that gun fire would not become a daily occurrence in Arroyo Loco.

A few moments later, and already in a hazy sleep, I heard the sound of a truck rumbling past, and few seconds after that, the whirring sound made by tires as it crossed our new bridge with the slip-proof metal prongs on the roadbed. None of this seemed worth giving up that last hour of sleep.

Later that same morning, and after a nice breakfast of Tia Carla's homemade *chorizos* and my scrambled eggs, I took my brand new binoculars and field guide outside. I spent about half an hour peering into the branches growing over my house. The new binoculars brought the tiny world of birds into such sharp focus, I felt like I was actually living in the trees with the chirping creatures. I saw yellow rumps on the yellow-rumped warblers, and the bright eyes on a blue and gray scrub jay. The American crow's feathers shimmered iridescent in the morning sun. I had just finished noting my new finds on my list and picked up my novel when Amanita came rushing down the hill at what had to be her top speed.

"Estela! Estela! Get your detective friend out here right now!" She stopped outside my screened porch and bent over, holding her knees and huffing. "Hurry!"

I didn't want to seem insensitive, but I thought it might be best if I learned what was distressing Amanita before I bothered Muñoz.

"What's the big emergency, Amanita?"

"They're gone! Everyone is gone from that house. The cars are all gone, and someone shot a bunch of holes in the front! Even that big front window is completely blown out! Didn't you hear the shots this morning?" She took aim with her finger. "Pow, pow ... pow, pow, pow! I couldn't believe no one even came to see what was happening!"

By this time, Bryce had arrived behind her. At least this morning his feet were attired in footwear intended to be worn outdoors. He ran a hand across his head, attempting to quell a particularly bad case of bed hair.

"Did you go up there, Amanita?" I asked.

"Well, yes. I waited, you know, until now, what with all that shooting. I heard a truck go by right after the shots. Then I waited until now to go look. Bullet holes, real bullet holes, Bryce!"

"Hmm." Sad day when our village is so inured to gunfire that we hardly even notice, let alone come running. I had to give Amanita her due. "Okay, that does sound like something Muñoz would be interested in knowing about."

"Wow!" Bryce said, finally getting the gist of Amanita's story. "I'm going up there to see!" He turned, prepared to run all the way.

106

"Whoa, Bryce!" I called. "The only thing we know for sure is that there was gunfire up there this morning. We should all stay away until the sheriff has a chance to check out what happened."

Bryce shifted, indecision wrinkling his brow. He usually objected to a girl telling him what to do.

"There could be bodies, Bryce."

He took two steps, still looking unconvinced.

"Dead bodies. I'll tell you what, Bryce. I'll go in right now and call the sheriff, and how about if you set up a perimeter, say, across the road in front of Amanita's place, and keep everyone behind that line until the detective gets here?"

Bryce's face momentarily clouded with disappointment. Then his officious side took over, and he puffed his chest out. "I'll get my baseball bat and get right on that," he called back over his shoulder, already on the way.

Muñoz was off somewhere on important other business, or maybe Saturday was his day off from answering phones. I had to leave a message. Investigating the by-now-probably-empty house might not be a huge priority, but as time ticked by and I waited for a return call, I started to wonder what important evidence might have been left behind.

After a solid twenty minutes waiting for Muñoz to return my call, I decided to take a walk up and at least look at the house from the point at which Bryce had established his road block. There wasn't much to see from the "command post" Bryce was "manning." He had set a broken wooden sawhorse at one edge of the road and a folding lawn chair at the other. In between, he'd lined up four faded orange plastic cones. They looked like something left over from when Bryce played soccer at the age of nine.

Finally getting smart in my middle-age, I had brought my binoculars along. Through those I could clearly see one of the large front windows shattered to smithereens. The front door was also pock-marked with what I took Amanita's word to be bullet holes, possibly inflicted using a semi-automatic weapon from the sounds I had heard. Either that, or the gunman had been very angry and firing rapidly.

After viewing that much, I was even more anxious to see what else might have been left behind. I considered my options. I was, after all, on the sheriff's dime as a consultant on this case. Maybe I could stretch that out to include investigating the apparently abandoned house. Where was that darned Muñoz when I needed him?

I peered again through the binoculars, focusing on each window, searching for movement, or any sign of someone still lurking inside. If there was someone there, they either weren't coming to the windows, or they couldn't. Wondered if someone might be in need of medical attention. I turned to Amanita, still hovering nearby. Her telephone was the closest.

"Amanita, I think we should call nine-one-one. There might be someone hurt inside that house. Can you do that, please?"

Her eyes grew large, and she disappeared inside, the screen door slamming behind her. She was back fifteen seconds later, holding her phone out to me.

"Really, Amanita?"

She pushed the phone toward me again. Not sure what her problem was, I took it and dialed. The harried dispatcher promised to send deputies out "as soon as possible," especially considering I was not able to ascertain whether there was an active shooter still on the scene.

I could, of course, have gone and looked myself, but it was the possibility that there might be someone rendered permanently incapable of movement that stopped me. I'm the sort of person who would do the right thing if someone needed to be rescued, which I felt like I had done by calling nine-one-one. But I'm also the sort of person who isn't that good at confronting scenes of possible bloody carnage.

I thought about the flowered flip-flops I'd seen on the stairs earlier. Where was Sissy? I took one step toward the house, Bryce bristling behind me. Then I had a second thought.

"Say, you guys, has either of you seen any signs of a dog up there? A really big dog?" They both shook their heads, no, and we all took another long look at the house. Even if the carnage was the dog, I didn't want to be the one to find it.

A sheriff's office K-9 unit arrived first, and wheeled up to Bryce's flimsy barricade. I explained about the gunshots and the report that the previous occupants of the house had abandoned ship. Amanita came up beside me and nodded earnestly, until she noticed the K-9 deputy in the back. A black shepherd, ears pointed forward, drool forming at the jaw.

"Eek!" Amanita squeaked and jumped backwards. "It's a dog!"

I wondered what she thought the "K-9 Stay Back" painted all over the SUV meant.

Bryce whisked away his orange cones before they could be flattened, and the vehicle rolled forward. By that time, a reasonably sized crowd of neighbors had gathered. Most of us settled on Amanita's steps where we could see at least part of the action. After he got parked, and from behind the cover of his heavy SUV, the deputy held up a bullhorn device and directed his message at the house.

"Sheriff's deputy here! Is there anyone inside the house?" No answer that we could hear. He tried again. "If you are inside the house, come out now. Hands over your head." Still no response. The deputy opened the rear door of his vehicle and let out the largest German shepherd I had ever seen.

"Ooh, look!" came Freda's squeal from behind me. "It is a German dog! That is a German dog."

Someone else mumbled an "uh-huh," but the rest of us were silent. I was mesmerized.

Holding the dog by the collar, the deputy moved closer to the front door, taking shelter behind the pillar on which the gate was mounted. He lifted his bullhorn again. "I have a K-9 here," he said, his voice transmitting urgency and impending danger. "I'm giving you three minutes, then I'm sending in the dog!"

In a hush, Helen whispered, "He's sending in the dog first? Doesn't that mean the dog will get shot first?"

"Yes." Something caught in my throat, and I didn't want to say more.

Helen went on. "That's how it works? The dog, who has no idea what might be in there, and what might happen to him, they send him in first to get shot?" Helen might be a keeper of cats, but that doesn't mean she doesn't also have room in her heart for dogs. She was turning purple. We watched as the deputy and his dog crept through the opening where the gate swung unlatched to the front step. The deputy pushed the door open with one hand, the other gripping his dog's collar.

"Yes," I said. "That is how it works. Dogs trust people, and trust that people wouldn't send them into danger, so they do whatever we ask."

"That's three!" the deputy yelled. "I'm sending in the dog, now!" He let go of the dog's collar, and the shepherd flew through the open doorway and disappeared inside.

"Search!" the deputy commanded, while waiting safely outside the entry. No sign of the dog. At least there were also no gun shots from inside.

Two sheriff's SUVs wheeled up to Bryce's barricade and Muñoz himself stepped out of the lead vehicle. I trotted over to meet him, hoping no one would choose that moment to let loose with a volley of bullets. With shock, I saw his usually spotless black loafers covered nearly to his socks with greenish mud and other less-identifiable gunk.

I let his less-than impeccable appearance slide, and explained about the dog now searching the house. Bryce reluctantly removed his plastic cones again.

Muñoz instructed the small crowd of neighbors to wait, out of the line of fire, until law enforcement had cleared the area. He gestured at me to follow him and patted the air, indicating that I should stay low. Surprising myself, I was too excited to be scared. The SUVs proceeded cautiously to the cul-de-sac in front of the house. Muñoz and I scuttled alongside, shielded from the house by the vehicle. Once it had parked, I stayed on the side away from the house, and peeped through the vehicle's windows when I wanted to see what was going on.

The deputies who'd been driving slipped out through the passenger doors. We all scanned the large residence from behind the cover of the vehicles, searching for any signs of movement or current occupation. The deputy who'd sent his dog inside stood on the porch, his ear cocked for the sound of any commotion inside. Nothing moved, not even so much as a curtain at an open window.

Three of the deputies began suiting up in tactical gear, body armor, helmets, shoulder-mounted radios, and heavy black flak jackets, and taking up ugly looking firearms. Even Muñoz slipped off his sports jacket and donned a tactical vest. Guess they forgot to bring one for me. Once the three deputies who would go first had collected and put on all their gear, they could hardly walk. They waddled toward the house, weapons at the ready.

The shepherd reappeared at the front door, looking for all the world as though he was disappointed at not finding any live bad guys. His handler gave him a good ruffling of the fur on his chest and fed him a handful of what I hoped were high-value treats. After all, even if the dog didn't know it, he had just risked his life for the taxpayers. The handler escorted his dog to the K-9 vehicle, clearing the stage for the tactically-attired deputies.

The entry gate swung lazily on its hinges when the first deputy gave it gentle push. The front door was also still slightly ajar. The black-clad figures crept toward the porch. They swept their guns across the front of the house, pausing at windows and behind pillars. The first guy reached out, slowly, ready to draw back at the slightest sign of danger. He pressed the doorbell button. We all heard it chime inside.

The dog had cleared the house. Even if someone had been hiding in a closet or anywhere else, the dog would have alerted. Guess the deputies did not entirely trust their K-9 friend yet.

We waited. Still hearing nothing. The deputy called into the house, again inviting anyone inside to present themselves. There was no response. I guess one can't be too careful if guns are involved.

The deputies moved forward again, one guy pushing the door fully open with a boot, and crossing the threshold. Once inside, they snapped into firing stance and disappeared into the dim interior. I had faith the dog had done his job, and knew their readiness to fire would not translate into accidentally shooting a dog, or a teenaged girl. As to shooting each other, they were on their own.

I whispered to Muñoz, both of us still hunkered behind an SUV. "Would the K-9 deputy have alerted to the dog inside? I mean, or would he greet the other dog? Should we have mentioned about the dog before the deputies went inside? Do those guys know there might be a big dog in there? Or maybe a teenage girl?"

He keyed on a radio attached to the shoulder of his tactical vest and relayed the information to the deputies now roaming the house. I leaned closer to his radio, hoping to hear the deputies calling "clear" as they went through each room, but maybe that's not something they really do.

After a few minutes we heard a lot of yelling from inside, and doors slamming. Finally, one of the upper windows slid open and the screen, a bullet hole shot through the middle, fell to the ground. A deputy stuck his head out.

"All clear. You can come on in." He didn't say anything about dead bodies or other random carnage.

Once on the front porch, Muñoz pulled on blue latex gloves and handed me a pair. Next, he lifted those shoe covers they wear on surgical wards out of his pocket and gave me a couple of those. We both gazed at his destroyed shoes. I wanted to ask what had happened, but now didn't seem like the time.

He asked me to wait outside for two seconds. After making a close-up examination of the front door with at least three bullet holes blown right through its heavy metal exterior, I wasn't entirely disappointed to be left on the stoop for a minute or two. I felt no call to be a hero in this situation.

The house had indeed been abandoned. Plates clotted with the remains of dried food filled the sink. Take-out containers and empty beer bottles cluttered the counters. The refrigerator was partially-stocked, although someone had removed some items, leaving behind a big space between the eggs and a half-filled pitcher of grape juice.

The rest of the rooms downstairs were mostly empty, not in a way indicating a move-out, but more as though they had never been furnished at all. Although trails of footprints tracked through the carpets, no trace of furniture feet were squashed into the deep pile. No paintings adorned the walls, no mail sat on the credenza, not so much as an abandoned tennis ball indicated the former presence of a dog.

In the otherwise empty living room, two small unframed certificates were propped prominently on the fireplace mantel. These turned out to be birth certificates. One was for a girl, born fifteen years ago in Seacaucus, New Jersey, and named Karen Marie Odam. The parents were listed as Yaxshi and Anya Odam. A tiny footprint attested to her healthy birth. The second certificate was for a boy, born eighteen years ago, also in Seacaucus, also with a footprint, and named Yaxshi Odam, Junior. Both certificates looked old, the card stock on which they were printed yellowed with age, a couple of the corners bent. Muñoz slid those into evidence envelopes with his gloved hands, and we examined them through the clear plastic. We scanned the empty room.

"Who leaves their kids' birth certificates propped on the mantle?" I said.

Muñoz huffed in a non-committal way.

"There's no pictures of the kids, just these."

Muñoz nodded, maintaining his silence.

"Still, this means the kids, even Chip, are really their biological children, right? So that boy in the morgue is their son? And if he's really their son, well, I think that significantly lessens the possibility that either of them had anything to do

114

with the boy's death. Although ...." I thought some more. "Although, that doesn't explain why they weren't more upset. Or why they denied that the body could be their son."

"Mother was upset."

"Yes, that's true, but not the father. And why did they insist the body was not Chip's?"

Muñoz rubbed his hand over his mouth as he gazed through the shattered front window.

"On the other hand," I said, beginning to feel like an annoying chatterbox, "these certificates sitting here like this ...."

"Uh-huh?"

"It's just a little too convenient, you know? Someone wanted us to see these."

"Yeah, but what does that mean?"

"I'm not sure, yet. I have to think."

We spent another hour wandering around the house. There was one rumpled bed upstairs. The Crime Scene Unit would collect the bedding and look for DNA. The other rooms had been emptied, leaving pock marks in the carpet where the legs of beds had stood. Maybe five or six people had been sleeping in the house. One room upstairs had been used as an office. Here we found a desk and bare table and clear imprints of other furniture in the carpet. Stray electrical cords, unplugged in a hurry, were scattered haphazardly around the floor. An empty wastebasket sat, tipped on its side. Whoever had done the moving must have gotten tired of hauling things down the stairs.

As we searched, I kept my eyes open for a telephone answering machine, but never saw one. There must have been one here if Roberto had left a message. Unless. I wandered until I ran across Muñoz again. "What if the phone number

Roberto called went to Odam's cell phone, and the message was left on Odam's cell phone voice mail?"

"Yeah?"

"Well, for one thing, that would significantly decrease the chance that anyone else, like those mobster goons, had heard the message."

"Yeah, and what does that mean?"

"I don't know, exactly, but it could be important."

Muñoz did not disagree.

CHAPTER TWELVE

Back downstairs, we sat on the fireplace hearth and waited for the evidence technicians to arrive with their fingerprint powder and camera equipment. At this point it appeared the only crime that had been committed was vandalizing the rental home, not a high priority for the county sheriff. The deputies dressed in tactical gear had all piled into one of the SUVs and taken off for other, more immediate and dangerous venues. The FBI was enroute, expected to arrive at any moment, and, according to Muñoz, royally pissed that they had not been notified earlier.

"I've been thinking about those birth certificates," I said.

Muñoz lifted his eyebrows in response.

"It's too convenient they were left there for us to find. Too convenient even that they exist. And I've been thinking, well ... remember, this Malakov guy is a skilled counterfeiter, and he reportedly makes false documents, identity papers and so on. So those birth certificates could be well-done fakes, couldn't they?"

Muñoz nodded. I could tell from his less-than-astonished expression that my thoughts were not a complete surprise to him.

"You think so, too?"

He lifted one shoulder and let it drop.

"Let me see those certificates again."

Muñoz spread the two pages in their plastic envelopes on the floor in front of us, and we bent over them. I picked up one, examining carefully the tiny inked footprint. Were our feet really ever that eensy? I put that one down and picked up the second one. I laid both side by side. When they were laid out like that, the flaw was obvious.

"Look at these footprints," I said.

Muñoz leaned over. After a minute he said, "They're the same."

"Exactly the same. The whole point of putting the baby's footprint on the birth certificate is identification, to distinguish one baby from another. These certificates have exactly the same footprint on both of them. It's not even that someone stamped one foot, inked it up again, and stamped it again. It is exactly the same print. These certificates are fake. I mean, it's probably not that easy to get the footprints of actual newborns to use on fake birth certificates, so Malakov had to use the same footprint on both."

"At least one of them is a fake."

"That's what I just said."

"No, you said they are both fakes."

"Oh. I get your point. Okay, one might be real. Damn, though, they both look so real, don't they?"

Muñoz pushed out his lips and nodded."

"This guy is good. How did he get the cards they're printed on to look so old?"

"Mystery to me."

I gazed around us, noting the shattered glass sparkling in the carpet. "So, what do you think happened here? I mean, somebody shot the place up, but why?"

"They were mad?"

"The mobsters, you mean. Here they got the Malakovs set up in this nice place with a new identity and then the family blows it and takes off?"

"Leaves the mob with this expensive set-up."

"Yes. Still, I don't see how shooting the place up is constructive in any way."

The detective turned and gave me a long stare.

"I know," I said. "Not everything people do is constructive, right?"

He bounced his eyebrows once, collected both evidence bags, and stood. He was still wearing the paper shoe covers, of course, and I noticed the seaweed again, now dried to a crisp olive-brown, and even caked up onto one black sock.

"So, what's the story with the muddy shoes? How did that happen?"

He looked at his shoes in disgust, then his face cleared. "We found the dinghy."

"Really? How? Where?"

"Put a notice in the on-line paper about it being stolen, possibly evidence in a murder investigation. A mother in Cayucos called us. Her boy and a couple of his friends found it hidden in a cove near Black Rock. We had to hike a couple of miles at high tide to get there, most of it through seaweed. The kids said they saw it when they were dirt-biking along the bluffs above."

The tone in his voice was skeptical.

"You don't believe them?"

"I think they did more than find it. Possibly took it for a joy ride and then hid it."

"You think these boys maybe had something to do with Chip's death?"

He shook his head, then said, "Possibly. They are about the same age as Chip. The mother says she's never met or even heard about a kid called Chip, but possibly the kids did know him. They went to school together. Dinghy is at the lab now. We'll see what we can get off it."

"So nothing else in the way of evidence?"

My phone jingled with the ditty I had programmed for all calls coming from my Arroyo Loco neighbors. Half a second later, a black sedan with tinted windows rolled into view out front. My breath caught in my throat. I hoped that black sedan was the FBI and not the returning mobsters. I answered the call. Bryce was on the phone, annoyed that the driver of the black vehicle had failed to be impressed with his roadblock, and had plowed right through. He whined that he'd barely had time to save his faded orange cones.

Out in the cul-de-sac, Agent Roybal climbed from his driver's seat. I assured Bryce he was doing a good job, especially by calling and letting us know, and it was okay for the FBI to go through his barricade.

That seemed to be the limit of what I could accomplish there, so I said my goodbyes to Muñoz. Wasn't much in the way of psychological forensic consulting I could provide now that the Malakovs and their friends had abandoned the scene. As I passed Amanita's porch, my neighbors began a disappointed grumbling, and I turned back to see several deputies decorating the fence all around the big house with bright yellow crime scene tape. I assured them there was nothing to see anyway and headed home to get started on that relaxing.

First though, there was lunch to consider. I've recently read that melons and bananas are good antidotes for heartburn triggered by stress, and there was plenty of that going around. I chopped hunks of fruit into a bowl and plopped a few large dollops of probiotic vanilla yogurt on top. Maybe I would add a small green salad later. Unlikely, but possible. I find it hard to eat and hold a book at the same time, so I sat on my porch and stared absently into space while munching.

Toward the end of my too-small meal, I became aware of rustling in the underbrush across the road. My new birding hobby has heightened my attention to the sounds of wildlife that surround me. This rustling did not sound so much like a robin as it did a rhinoceros. I considered going inside, just in case one of Malakov's mean-looking friends had been left behind. Shiner and Scout, who napped at my feet, both looked up, staring hard toward the source of the rustling. A low growl started deep in Shiner's throat. Scout got up and retreated through the dog door. The hackles on Shiner's neck stood straight up. He looked about ready to tear right through the screen and attack whatever was over there. I put him inside, too, and closed the door dog. Injured dogs I do not need.

I stepped back and was just easing over to pick up my binoculars when the black snout appeared. Not taking my eyes off it, I sat down. Shiny black eyes peered at me from under a leaf. She moved her head slightly, pushing the branches aside, and we regarded one another in a long stare.

Reddish-brown fur covered most of her head, and a large brown hump rose on her back, making her look more like a small buffalo. I'm not going to say she was pretty, but her face definitely had character. She huffed at me, took another step, then slid down the slight embankment and onto the road. Much, much larger than I had pictured our wild boar, she lifted her flat snout and appeared to be sampling the air for my scent. I held perfectly still, ready to dash behind the kitchen door if necessary, although as big as she was, she would have been more than able to crash right through, should she have so desired.

I'm calling this animal a female because, once her whole body was in view, I could see teats on her belly. Somewhere, not too far away, a litter of boarlets, or piglets, or whatever they are called, waited for her safe return.

That was the main reason I didn't call Grant, or anyone else with a gun. Here she was, just trying to live a boar's life, trying to get enough to eat so she could feed her babies. I'm sure she was just as disturbed to find me inhabiting her grazing grounds as I was to find her wandering my neighborhood. Although boar are apparently not in any imminent danger of extinction, I did not want to be personally responsible for the starvation and death of a nearby nest of piglets.

The rumbling of at least one vehicle started up on the road above us. The mother boar and I both glanced that way. I stepped into my kitchen, and by the time I got Shiner off the dining room table where he had climbed for a better view of the unusual wildlife, my friend the boar had vanished into the underbrush.

I could have gone out to the porch, and waved down Muñoz as he left the scene, but that had been one very large boar. I decided to give her time to wander farther away, while the dogs and I stayed inside. I could use the time to research wild boar on the computer. It turned out there was a lot I didn't know on the subject.

The dusk of late afternoon in the canyon had fallen when I finally looked up. Guess I was going to be on my own for dinner. I rummaged through the frost-encrusted contents of my freezer and decided to combine my trip to round up Inez's sheep for the night with a hunting and gathering foray to the local natural food store. Maybe I would even treat myself to some take-out Chinese from Mee Heng Low Noodle House in town.

I made it as far as Freda's house before being flagged down by Helen, standing in the middle of the road. I could see where this business of blocking traffic could get out of hand. Lowering my window, I left the ignition running.

"Might as well pull over, 'Stel'. We've got another neighborhood emergency."

"Really, Helen? Now? I have stuff I need to do."

"Estela, you know how these people here can get out of control without your calm voice of reason." I found Helen's comment a bit obsequious, since she herself was the most likely neighbor to fly off the handle in a crisis. A huge exasperated sigh on my part did nothing to placate her, so I pulled into Delia's driveway and parked. Freda's front porch was crowded with the usuals, Nina and Lauren, as well as Freda and Helen. Lauren scooted over on a step to make room and I sat down.

"So, what's the big emergency?" I said.

"It is these boar," Freda said. "Or rather, not these poor boar, but the people with the guns who want to shoot them." We all shared sad nods. "They will miss no doubt, and shoot one of us!"

"*Si*," Nina agreed, "Or one of the children, or our pets."

Helen, who had been cruising around with her husband Grant and his shotgun the other night, had another thought. "What are we going to do, though? We can't just let the boar overrun the neighborhood. They rooted up the Carper's whole front yard last week!"

"I just read they kill and eat small mammals, too," I added. "If we let the boar stay, we'll lose our other wildlife."

"Ah," Lauren said, "not to mention Helen's cats."

Helen blanched.

"But your cats are always in the house, right Helen?" I said. "Everyone knows how dangerous it is to let cats roam unsecured."

"Sure, yes ...." Helen said, still not regaining her color. I had to admit, the idea of a boar killing and eating a cat made me feel a tad faint as well. And when I thought about how large my new friend the mother boar was, and how possible it might be for her to crash through my newly installed fence to get to my dogs, the idea of running the boar off to some other location gained in appeal.

"Is there some way we can get rid of them without shooting them?" I said. "We don't want a lot of guys with guns shooting up the neighborhood, and anyway, I read that boar are among the most intelligent animals in the world. They quickly learn to avoid hunters, and they also reproduce so fast that hunting does little to decrease the population. Plus, their piglets are just so darned cute."

We sat in silence for a bit. I, personally, was picturing a bloody boar massacre.

"Some places have programs to cut down on feral cat populations by capturing, spaying, and releasing the cats," Helen said.

"Ah, yes, I've heard where they do something similar with mosquitoes," Lauren said. "You know, treat and release infertile mosquitoes."

"Those boar are huge," I said. "I'm having a hard time picturing the catch, spay, and release of even one boar, let alone the dozen or so we seemed to have roaming Arroyo Loco." That got more nods.

"Yes, that does seem unlikely." Freda agreed. "Do they also have those ...?" she gestured here, stroking something imaginary at the corners of her mouth.

"Mustaches?" Helen teased.

"Ah, tusks?" Lauren said.

"Those are actually their canine teeth, not the same as tusks," I informed everyone.

Helen gazed down at me with a haughty expression.

"What?" I said, "I've been reading about them."

"Whatever those things are, I should think they would be quite dangerous," Freda said. "I don't think we should try to capture the boars."

"Possibly shoot them with a tranquilizer gun?" Helen took aim with her finger.

"Ah, yes! What about a drug?" Lauren asked. "I could look it up, see if there is some drug we could feed them to prevent reproduction."

"That's definitely worth looking into," I said. As cute as those piglets were in the photographs, I was not opposed to preventing the birth of more. "In the meantime, they respond well to being chased off with loud noises. Maybe if we bang pans at them whenever we see them, we can convince them Arroyo Loco's not the place they want to live."

"Hey, 'Stel' speaking of noise, tell us what happened up at the big house this morning. What was all that racket about earlier? Sounded like gunshots. Grant said someone was using a semi-automatic rifle on the boar."

With that, we were off to the races with another twenty minutes of me explaining about the mobsters shooting up the big house. I had previously mentioned to Freda about finding the boy's body, but the rumor mill had done it's darnedest to tangle the story. It seemed best at that point to set the record straight.

"And how about that, 'Stel'?" Helen was full of questions this afternoon. "Did you ever figure out where that body came from?"

"Oh, that had to be those mobsters, don't you think?" Freda said. "Those guys are always killing each other."

Nina looked confused. "I thought it was a boy on the beach, not a mobster. Why would mobsters kill a young boy? Wasn't he the son of the family living in the big house?"

Helen jumped in. "Yeah, but Nina, think about it. He's the son of a family of criminals. He lives with criminals, and not just some low-life burglars, but organized crime-type criminals. I mean, they might have been friendly enough to us, but those were serious bad guys we met. It only makes sense they would be the ones committing serious crimes, like murder."

"And now they are gone." Freda rubbed her hands together, then clasped them to her mouth. "Now they are gone, thank goodness for that."

I had to admit, that explanation made for a neat package. Even if it meant Chip's killers would never be found, at least they were gone and no longer posed any danger to us. The FBI could worry about them, and we could go back to life as usual in our semi-peaceful hamlet.

"So that's that, then?" Helen said. "The mobsters killed the son and now they've taken off and disappeared?" She arched her eyebrows at me.

Why does everyone think I always have the answers? I shrugged. "Maybe. Say, here's a question. There was a teenage girl in that house, too. I saw her there myself. But she wasn't in the car with the parents when they took off, and she's not in the house now. Did anyone see her leave? Maybe in one of those black cars? This would have been any time between late Wednesday and early this morning?"

All I got were blank looks. There'd probably been numerous trips in black cars over that long a period in time. No one could remember anything specific. "Well, ask around when you get a chance. Maybe one of the other neighbors saw her leave."

We all agreed that Lauren would look into the possibility of some kind of birth control for boar, and we'd meet again when she had more information. I was at last permitted to go on my way, and high time, too. I picked up my Chinese food, hit the market, and barely made it out to the sheep ranch to bring in the flock before darkness fell.

Everything had gone well the evening before, so I had no reason to expect any problems that second evening. And for the most part, there really were no problems. Both the clicker and my personal count recorded forty six sheep, one more than there should have been. I tried to verify by counting after they entered the arena, but what with all of the milling around, I wasn't having much luck. Not only that, but on my third try I realized I was accidentally including at least one Pyrennes dog in my count. Reasoning that the clicker's indication that one extra sheep had entered the arena for the night was better than finding one too few sheep, I called it done and headed home.

CHAPTER THIRTEEN

After having been rudely awakened the previous several mornings, you would think I would have let myself sleep in on Sunday morning. Sadly, that was not to be. I'd read through those brochures from the bird store, and signed up for an early morning birding walk.

My very first official birding expedition. I had resolved to keep my mouth shut so as not to reveal my ignorance, and for the most part, that worked. The other birders and I met up with our leader in the parking lot for the San Simeon Trail, and headed off across the boardwalk there to look for birds around the creek.

The first thing I learned on this trip was that birds are a lot more sensible than the humans who seek them out. Birds tend to stay peacefully sleeping on branches until the sun comes out and warms the air a bit. We did not see a darn thing for the first hour. Next time maybe I'll show up an hour late.

We tried the trail alongside the wetlands, where every six feet or so, one person or another stopped us all to try to get our binoculars focused on something exciting. This usually turned out to be a knob on a piece of driftwood sticking out of the reeds.

Two people got left behind completely, locked in a heated debate about whether they had spotted a long-billed dowitcher or a short-billed dowitcher. They set up expensive-looking spotting scopes and continued their argument while peering through those. Apparently the length of the bill is not what distinguishes the two dowitchers.

I ambled along with the remaining birders, and as we climbed the hill at the south end of the wetlands, we were treated to the screams of a red-tailed hawk overhead. At least that's what everyone else said it was. I dutifully wrote that down on my list, but put a little x by it, since I had not seen the actual bird.

Farther along the trail, I dropped behind to focus on a bird hopping though the underbrush. Settling on a nearby bench, I got the binoculars focused on the spot. About the size of a robin, with a long beak. It appeared to be digging in the dirt. I'm not that familiar with my new field guide yet, so I tried to look the bird up on my phone bird identification app.

Crunching footsteps alerted me to a woman tromping toward me on the trail. She plopped on the bench beside me.

"Where's the rest of the group?"

"Oh, they went on ahead. I wanted to get this bird." Already I'd learned to "get" a bird means to identify it, and add it to your list.

She nodded while digging out her binoculars. "I always come an hour late," she said. "No sense in getting here before the birds are even awake."

I had to laugh. A woman after my own heart.

"Emily," she said, holding out her hand.

I introduced myself.

"So what do you think that is?" Emily asked, peering at the bird under the bushes.

I pointed at a picture on my phone app. "I was thinking maybe a hoopoe? See how it's foraging under the bushes?"

"Well, it is about the right size, so possibly, but you know the hoopoe is a European and North African bird. If it is a hoopoe, it's quite aways off course."

Time to come clean. "I don't have any idea really. I'm new at this."

"Good!" she said. "I like someone who can admit their limitations. That was a good start at identifying that bird, noticing its size and behavior. Next, you need to check the range map. Lots of times a bird might look like one thing, but from the range map you can tell that species would never be where you're thinking it is, so what you're looking at must be something else. I think what you've got there is a hermit thrush."

I flipped my field guide open to the thrush page. Field guides are much easier to use if you already have a name for the bird and just need to confirm your identification. Sure enough, that appeared to be a hermit thrush.

"They're shy," Emily said, "so you rarely see them. Good spotting."

That made me happy. At the same time, I could see where learning to be a birder was going to take a lot of practice. Feeling smug, I noted my find on my day's checklist. Emily, breathed a heavy sigh and hoisted herself off the bench.

"Catch up with you next time." She waved as she continued out the trail.

I sat on the bench a while longer, thinking about my out-of-range hoopoe. Drifting back to the topic of Chip who had lived in Arroyo Loco, but was found dead on the beach in Cayucos. And the dinghy taken from the Poddelka moored south of Morro Bay, but found hidden a couple of miles north of Cayucos. Both Chip and the dinghy were found out of their ranges. What did that mean? And their paths crossed in Cayucos. Was there meaning hidden in that fact, as well?

The sun had burned off the fog by then, and the day was warming rapidly. I had added six birds to my list, more than doubling the number of species. Time to head home for lunch.

I tried to get into my novel, but after ten minutes or so, I realized I was not in the mood to read. Just as well, too, because a few seconds later, the phone rang, Muñoz's name in the display.

He asked if I might be interested in seeing the place on the bluff where the boys said they'd seen the dinghy. He also wanted me to accompany him to interview the one boy whose mother had called with the information. Knowing this expedition would entail a walk of a couple of miles, I considered. I've given up my membership at the gym, since it was costing me a significant amount each month, and mostly only inducing guilt about not going, so I'm always looking for an excuse to go for a walk. I left Scout asleep in his bed, loaded Shiner onto the back seat, and met the detective in the parking lot of the Piggly Wiggly in north Morro Bay.

Muñoz blinked rapidly in surprise when I opened the back door of his sedan and popped Shiner inside, but I've learned to ignore driver's howls of protest. What's he going to do back there, shed? Besides, it's not like that already battered sedan was going to be damaged any more by the presence of a dog. For his part, Shiner was right at home behind the wire grill, and at least that way he couldn't plant unappreciated slurps on Muñoz's cheek.

As we drove, Muñoz explained that the boys claimed to have found the small boat hidden in a cove, and one had told his mother when she remarked after reading about the sheriff's search. We cruised into Cayucos and parked at the end of

Ocean Avenue where a dirt parking lot gave access to the trails along the headlands. Behind us, cattle dotted the hills belonging to the ranchers around Harmony and Sparrow Ranch. Ahead of us stretched the grassy headlands and the vast expanse of the Pacific ocean beyond.

Shiner raced out the trail toward the ocean, his black and white tail pin-wheeling in excitement. I called him back. Along that stretch, the headlands end in an abrupt drop, fifty feet or more, to the rocky beach below. Muñoz and I came within ten feet or so of the edge, stepped off the trail, and crept carefully forward until we could see the bottom of the cliff. He pointed to a small cove nestled into the base.

"That's where the boys said they found the dinghy, hidden back in there."

"Really," I said. Not a question, more like a statement. "Didn't you say the boys were riding their bikes up here when they found it?"

"That's what they said."

"So, how did they see it? Especially if they were on bikes?" I searched the ground at my feet. Although the damp dirt readily took imprints, even Shiner's paws were leaving tracks, and the zig-zag pattern on the bottom of my running shoes was clear, there were no signs of bicycles having passed here any time recently. "They would have had to have gotten off the bikes at just this point, crept to the edge like we are doing, and leaned way over. Even then, they'd have to have known exactly where to look."

"Yep."

"If they actually did see the boat from up here, they must have already known it was there."

The detective crinkled his forehead at me.

"Maybe they were walking down there on the beach at low tide and they saw it."

"Kind of rocky along there. Not the place for a walk, unless it was low tide."

"Right. Maybe they were out in another boat and saw it?"

"Then why not just tell the truth? Why tell us they saw it from up here?"

"I don't know. Their story seems unlikely, that's all, and makes me wonder about the real story."

"Let's go talk to the boy," he said. "We'll ask him."

We didn't have any trouble finding the address Muñoz had gotten from the mother. The house was on a steep hill overlooking Cayucos. This being the beginning of summer vacation from school, five teenagers, girls as well as boys, lounged on and around the concrete steps leading up from the driveway. They turned sullen expressions on us when the dark sedan pulled up. Muñoz got out and, in a friendly enough manner, flashed his identification. A couple of the girls rose and started gathering belongings, preparing to leave. Then I let Shiner out of the car.

The atmosphere suddenly changed as Shiner approached the group, a wide dog-grin lighting his face. His tail waved a sociable hello, and wagged faster when two of the kids came forward, oohing as they greeted the happy dog. Muñoz disappeared up the steps, presumably to introduce himself to the parents. I stayed with the teenagers answering questions about Shiner while everyone who cared to got a chance to pet his soft coat.

From my position on the steps of the posh house on the hill, I gazed over the small town of Cayucos. Unlike in parts of California, where the expensive houses are lined up along the beach, in Cayucos the beach front properties are mostly shanties and old motels, with the showy houses built on the hill above. I looked south and realized, if I had my binoculars with me I could have brought Evan's bungalow into clear view. And there he was, or someone, a tiny figure moving along the side of his house. From this distance, it was hard to be certain who it was out there. Peering, my hand shading my eyes, I tried to make out what he was doing. Maybe digging? Possibly burying something in that narrow side yard? Couldn't really tell. It did look like he had a shovel or some kind of a tool.

"Does this dog do anything?" one of the kids asked. "Would he chase a ball or anything?"

I showed them pictures on my phone of Shiner herding sheep. Even the boys seemed impressed with Shiner's athletic achievements. I explained the mud and sand on Shiner's paws by saying we had just been out looking at the spot where they, or some of them, had been when they'd seen the dinghy. "You know," I said, "In that cove where it was hidden?" No one said anything, but a couple of them shot glances at one another. Not sure what, if anything, to make of that.

Coming down the steps, Muñoz looked around. "Kevin?" No one responded. Muñoz took a deep breath. I could tell he was preparing to let loose with one of his exasperated sighs.

"Hey, guys," I said, "We just had a question about finding that dinghy."

"We all found it together," one of the girls said, and the kids drew almost imperceptibly closer.

"Yeah, I know Kevin wasn't the only one," Muñoz said. "But I need permission from each of your parents before I can ask you questions. So far, I've only gotten permission from Kevin's parents. Which one of you is Kevin?"

"He's the one in the ratty red tee shirt," an angry voice came from above, where a woman leaned out an open window.

134

"And when the sheriff is done with you, young man, you can march yourself right up here and deal with me." Muñoz must have mentioned to her that Kevin could not have been being entirely truthful when he said they saw the dinghy from the headland trail.

This was not going so well. All of the kids lowered their brows, as though by doing so they could block their rapidly reddening faces from from the glare of their companion's mother. The boy in the ratty red tee shirt shuffled forward, shooting an angry scowl at Muñoz.

The detective gestured encouragingly. "Over here, son." Muñoz attempted to draw Kevin away from his friends. They got maybe three steps away before the other boy stepped forward to join them.

"I just need to talk to Kevin right now," Muñoz said.

"You said you only had permission to ask Kevin the questions," the other boy answered. "You never said we couldn't all listen."

Muñoz shot me a glance, but the boy had a point. I shrugged. At the same time, I could see the dilemma Muñoz faced. The kids had told him a convoluted and unlikely to be entirely true story about the dinghy. If they knew the questions he was going to ask before he had permission to talk to each of them alone, they would have plenty of time to coordinate their stories.

Muñoz sighed. "Okay, then. How many of you were there when you found the dinghy? Show of hands?" All five kids raised their hands. The detective scowled. One girl sheepishly lowered her hand. "Are you sure there were four of you there?" They cut glances among themselves. The other girls dropped their hands. "Okay, then, just you two boys?"

No one replied. "And how many of you knew Chip Odam from school?" This time all the hands went up and stayed up. Muñoz pulled out his notebook and a pen and began collecting names and contact information from everyone. We thanked them. I popped Shiner into the back seat and we left the kids in the driveway where we'd found them.

As we merged onto the highway, Muñoz pulled a plastic bag from his jacket pocket and dropped it on the console.

"What's that?"

"Kevin's mother found it in his jeans when she did the laundry. Just the capsule. She put it in the baggy."

I looked more closely. Sure enough, there was a clear gelatin capsule filled with white powder inside the bag.

"So, what do you think it is?"

"Let's the lab decide. There's no writing on it. It looks homemade."

I sat in quiet contemplation for a mile or two, gazing across the beach to the indigo ocean beyond. "Have you thought about the fact that Chip was found here in Cayucos and the dinghy was also found here? Neither one of those belonged here." I shifted to look at Muñoz. He chewed the inside of one cheek. Taking another tack, I went on. "You know, at least during the summer, there's probably not much that happens along this stretch of coast that those teenagers don't know about."

"And your point?"

"I'm only suggesting that if we can manage not to alienate them, they might be helpful in sharing what they know, or at least keeping their eyes open for anything new." We were passing south Cayucos as I spoke, and I imagined Evan sitting out on his deck with his binoculars trained on the beach. "In fact, it's possible someone we've never talked to saw something that might help us figure out what happened."

"*Es verdad*," he mumbled. "What are you suggesting?"

"I don't know, exactly. I guess just that we try to stay in the information-gathering phase for a while longer before we get into the drawing-conclusions phase."

He nodded. "I'll get a deputy to contact the parents, set up interviews."

"Ask the kids about parties on the cabin-cruiser, too," I suggested.

"With their parents right there?"

"Oh, yes, unlikely they'd say anything, huh? Hmm."

CHAPTER FOURTEEN

A deep June gloom buried the coastal hillsides Monday morning when I pulled into Inez's ranch. She had returned the night before, long after Shiner and I had put her sheep away for the night. She and her dog had added numerous ribbons and new titles to their collection.

The work never ends at a sheep ranch. In addition to running a dog-day-care kennel, training herding dogs and their handlers, and breeding border collie puppies, Inez also sells the high-quality wool produced by her small herd of Merino sheep. That Monday morning was the day all forty-five sheep would be sheared for the summer.

The flock were finishing their bales of alfalfa and becoming restive at being shut in the arena when I arrived. They were accustomed to being released to the hillsides early in the morning, and several of them were bleating their dismay. I scooted Shiner and Scout into one of the day-care kennels, as their help would not be needed, and made my way out to the far gate.

Inez and her helpers had arranged hog panels to create an escape-proof pen outside the gate and a crew of four professional shearers were busily setting up their equipment. Once they were ready, Inez and her dog started the slow process of separating two of the ewes at a time from the flock.

By nature, sheep try to stay close to one another and move together. The dog's job is to cut through the flock, and separate two ewes from the rest. This is called "cutting." After several tries, Inez and her dog succeeded in cutting two sheep, and moving them to the gate. Those were released to the small pen, where the shearers took charge. Each one turned a sheep onto her back, and snuggled the animal between taut knees. Worried the sheep might be scared or hurt, I watched closely, but the opposite seemed to be true. The animals were mostly calm, and showed all signs of being glad to be rid of their heavy wool coats. The wool came off almost in one piece. Inez came to stand beside me.

"They don't even look scared," I said.

Inez laughed. "About as scared as a poodle being groomed. That wool is quite a burden by now, and they don't want it in the summer. Plus, being sheared makes for a healthier flock, and cleaner lambing conditions." She pointed out one ewe with a swollen belly being let back into the arena. Eight of the ewes were bred and due to give birth in the next couple of weeks. Each one of those got a special coat buttoned over her—my job —and was allowed to return to an enclosure close to the barn where she could munch more energy-rich alfalfa.

After I'd put the warming coats on the pregnant ewes, Inez assigned me the job of gathering up the sheared wool and stuffing it into huge white canvas bags, ready for the wool-buyer. No matter how much wool I stuffed into a bag, there always seemed to be room to stuff in a little more. That was hard work.

In between tasks, I watched Inez and her dog cut two more sheep from the flock. That's what we need to do with those teenagers, I thought. We need to cut each one from the flock and get their individual stories. Might need to cut them from their parents, too, if we wanted to get the real story. I should mention that to Muñoz, although probably he was already aware of that particular insight.

I let my mind wander back to our problem in Arroyo Loco with the boar. Began to wonder if maybe the dogs could help out with that problem. The next time I drifted close enough to Inez to inquire, I explained, and asked abut maybe having the dogs round up the boar.

"Bad idea," she said. "Your average adult feral pig can weigh upwards of five hundred pounds, with an aggressive nature. Too smart to be intimidated by a silly barking dog. Feral pigs would kill your dog as soon as look at him."

So much for that idea. I made a mental note to keep my dogs away from our visitors.

Even with all the help, shearing forty-five ewes took most of the day. On the way home, I swung by that new healthy Mexican place to load up on takeout food. I was not in the mood to cook for myself. This time I actually made it all the way home without interruption. I thought about diving into that novel while I ate, but realized it had been days since I'd looked at my email. Better catch up on that first.

And, wouldn't you know, the first message that popped up was an announcement with the subject line "Emergency HOA Meeting." The meeting was to take place that very evening, and the topic was proposed methods for the eradication of the wild boar in Arroyo Loco. Because it was scheduled to start later than usual, it would not be preceded by a community potluck, for which I, for one, was grateful. Somedays it's all I can do to feed myself, and even that might consist of a dinner of breakfast cereal. Happy not to have to think of and prepare an acceptable potluck contribution, I forked up my takeout food and finished reading the waiting emails.

140

Muñoz called as I was finishing a quick washing up in the kitchen. He'd met individually with the parents and every one of the five teenagers connected with finding the dinghy, and who'd said they had known Chip. Not too surprisingly, not one of the kids had anything to add to their previous reports. The most common response he got to any of his questions was "I don't know," followed closely by, "I don't remember." I pointed out that he might have gotten better luck if he'd been able to speak with the teenagers outside the presence of their parents. I will not quote his response here. Suffice to say, he did not find my comments enlightening.

About the only productive outcome of the interviews he conducted that day had been the collection of fingerprints and DNA samples from each of the kids. In fact, he said, his interviews had been so blatantly unhelpful, he had already gotten permission from three of the parents to interview their children at the sheriff's substation without the parents present.

"I had to tell them there would be a psychologist present during the interviews," he said. "Not that they don't trust me. Just, the idea of a psychologist helped them feel more comfortable, especially a psychologist from the university counseling center. When can you do it?"

I gazed longingly at my novel. I'd started it numerous times, and never made it past page four. I reluctantly agreed to meet with him and whoever he could schedule in the morning.

I played briefly with my dogs, then secured them inside the house. Until this boar situation was resolved, I needed to keep them safe, either with me, or indoors. Certain members of the community had seen fit to pass rules about dogs attending our meetings, and I wasn't in the mood to argue after the long day I'd had. I started off on foot for the roadhouse at the junction of Arroyo Loco Road and the highway.

Freda was coming down her porch steps bearing a covered platter as I passed, so I held up and we walked together as far as Helen's.

"How's that mole on your leg, Freda? Did you see a doctor about that?"

"Oh, yes, Estela." An embarrassed expression flashed across her face and she waved one hand dismissively, tipping the loaded platter precariously. "It is not cancer. It is nothing. That is probably why your dogs could not smell it."

Too tired to provide a more educational explanation, I only nodded. Helen joined us, with Grant trudging along behind carrying a fragrant casserole dish. We'd made it as far as the bridge when Lauren came trotting up behind us, waving a few pages of printing and carrying a baggie of fresh vegetable sticks.

"Ah, good evening," she said. "I found that information we wanted. You know, about a drug that can be given to make the boar infertile."

I was relieved to have the possible option of a non-lethal solution to our problem, and looked forward to hearing more about it. By the time we had added Nina and her bowl of chicken wings to our group, we still had fifteen minutes before the meeting. We busied ourselves setting chairs up in a circle, more chairs than usual, since these emergency meetings generally garner more interest than the average business meeting. After a bit of fumbling, Nina and Helen, who are not our usual coffee-makers, got the pot going. Freda uncovered her platter to reveal a mound of finger-sized crescents dusted with powdered sugar. They looked delicious. I didn't want to be the first to snatch one because there was that powdered sugar to consider. If I took the first cookie and slipped it into my mouth, everyone would see the sugar on my fingers, and even probably smeared around my mouth. I waited politely until Grant had helped himself to two or three.

"*Vanillekipferl*," Freda said. "Please, have two. They are small."

"Neil who?" Helen said, piling three on a napkin.

"*Vanillekipferl*, Helen," Freda corrected. "They are vanilla crescents."

Helen wandered away, muttering something about Mrs. Kipferl and her son, Neil. She wasn't gone for long though, as she was back five minutes later for a few more *vanillekipferl*, her upper lip dusted with white.

As predicted, over the next several minutes many more residents than usual entered the roadhouse meeting room and settled into the circled chairs. Most of them carried platters, which they added to the growing collection on the table in back. I leaned over to my friend, Nina.

"I thought this wasn't going to be a potluck. Why is everyone bringing food?"

"It's not a potluck, Estela. It's finger-food. Someone suggested we bring finger-food."

"It looks like a potluck to me."

She shrugged. "Help yourself, Estela. There's lots of food."

Great, I thought. Just what I need. Two dinners. I resolved to resist, at least within the context of I had already eaten several of those delicious *vanillekipferl*.

By the time our HOA President, Graciela Garcia, called the meeting to order we were standing room only, and I didn't even recognize several of those in attendance. One pugnacious-looking guy, dressed in camouflage combat fatigues and a green beret, stood in the corner.

He turned out to be the representative of a local militia. They were raising money for their "tactical operations" by contracting out to private parties to conduct "search out and eradicate missions on unwanted and bothersome animal life." His words made my face hot and my stomach turn over.

No one ever admitted inviting Mr. Militia Man to our meeting, but after a long cold silence, he was asked to leave. If anyone was going to be permitted to go around Arroyo Loco shooting guns, we would all prefer they be our residents, however inept they might prove to be. At least we could have some degree of confidence our own people might know the difference between a marauding feral pig and Sunshine's beagle Itches running loose.

The idea of a small army stalking through Arroyo Loco with high-powered weapons sent a chill through the room, and put everyone off the idea of shooting our boar. After someone asked what we would do with all the dead bodies, the suggestion about putting out bowls of poison also received a cool response.

All in all, we are a fairly live-and-let-live crowd. The boar could be scary, and the few neighbors who tried to add a bit of landscaping around their homes were frustrated, but no one wanted to go overboard with our response. As we discussed it, the main issue seemed to be that, even if we were willing to tolerate the presence of a few boar, the few would all too soon become many. The atmosphere in the room was perfect for the introduction of Lauren's proposal to control boar fertility.

Of course, we might have known nothing would be that easy. First, it turned out, the infertility drug was expensive, and the Arroyo Loco Homeowner's Association Emergency Fund had been completely depleted by the construction of our new bridge, road, and sidewalks. As much we appreciated those amenities, and even with the financial assistance of state funds, we would still be paying for those for decades. The cost of four hundred dollars for the infertility drugs, and professionals to administer them, was just not in our budget.

Discussions about passing the hat, or individual household assessments had been going on for twenty minutes when a grumbling on one side of the circle erupted into a call for attention. It was Christopher. He and his wife Jessica and their four small boys had recently moved into the Carpers' place and were almost finished with a major remodel. In my experience so far, they had both done a good deal more complaining than contributing. We settled down to hear their input, but, predictably, instead of helping, they chucked in another monkey wrench.

"We don't believe in birth control," Christopher said, with Jessica, much shorter, beside him nodding energetically.

Helen turned a scowl their direction. "What do you mean you don't 'believe in' birth control, Christopher? Do you mean you don't believe it exists? Or you don't believe it works to prevent pregnancy? Because I can lay your mind to rest. It does exist, and it does work." One of the things I like about Helen, is that she does not suffer fools gladly. "Perhaps what you meant to say is that you don't think using birth control is right for you."

Christopher shifted uncomfortably in his flimsy folding chair. "We're not comfortable with using or paying for birth control."

There was an unusual moment of silence in our meeting room.

Still feigning ignorance, Helen said, "No one is saying you have to use birth control, Christopher." A voice from somewhere behind the circle on the other side muttered something along the lines of "closing the barn door after the horse has run," which got a few chuckles. I may have

145

mentioned Christopher and Jessica already have four small boys, and if I am not mistaken, that bump Jessica was sporting could be the sign of another on the way.

A good sense of humor was clearly not among Christopher's strongest characteristics. He turned an unfriendly face toward the voice. "As I said, I am not comfortable with the use of birth control. Or paying for it."

Freda turned on her sweetest smile and leaned forward. "But Christopher, these are pigs. We will use birth control on pigs only."

Christopher pushed his long body back in the folding chair, always risky, and crossed his arms. "Birth control is birth control, and I'm not comfortable."

As I may have said earlier, I'm never sure how someone telling me they are not comfortable gets translated into me having to accommodate them. The way I see it, if they're not comfortable, that's their problem, which they can solve by getting over it. Those boar had done more damage to Christopher's landscaping than almost anyone else's, and Christopher had done plenty of complaining about it. I couldn't see where him being uncomfortable with our solution was an issue about which we had to be concerned.

"And we don't think anyone else should use it either," Jessica said in her little-girl whine.

This set off a whole raft of shifting, squeaking chairs. Glances shot back and forth around the circle as we wondered which of us was going to step into the middle of this increasingly awkward discussion. It began to look as though no one else was up for the profiles-in-courage moment. Again, it would be up to me.

"Well, Christopher and Jessica, you are free to choose what you think is right for you, but you are not free choose what is right for other people."

Jessica started to interrupt with something about "the babies" but I kept talking.

"So, pretty much what I'm hearing you say here," I said in as polite a tone as possible, "is that you don't want to chip in money?" Christopher pulled his lips tight, and his face grew red by degrees, but he said nothing more. "Okay then, let's move on."

I turned back to Lauren. "Could we save any money, maybe by buying the drugs and administering them ourselves?" It was just a thought, and judging by the puzzled faces around the room, I wasn't the only one having trouble imagining how we might do that.

"What do you mean, Estela?" Raymond asked. "Could we use your dogs to round them up?"

"No, no, the dogs are not going to be any help with the boar," I said "I'm just trying to think how we could save some money."

"Ah ... " Lauren said, "the cost of the drug includes a technician to administer it. The lab will not sell just the drug."

"Well, that's a nuisance," Helen said. "Why not?"

I had to laugh. "It's probably like bed bugs, Helen." No one had any idea what I was talking about, so I had to explain. "Some dog handlers train their dogs to alert to the smell of bed bugs. It's a useful talent. Whenever you check into a hotel, particularly the kind of hotel that would let you have your dog in the room, your dog can check for bed bugs."

"By sniffing, you mean?" said Nina.

"Yes, and alerting if they smell bed bugs."

"Seriously? That sure beats what they tell you to do, you know, take the sheets off, inspect the mattress, look in all the places the maid hasn't cleaned in months. Who does all that?" She scanned the circle. "I want a bed-bug sniffing dog."

"Well, Nina, as much as I think you having a dog is a great idea, you won't be able to train a dog to alert to bed bugs because it's no longer legal to sell live bed bugs to anyone who does not have a professional pest inspection license."

"Wait! Let me guess," Marla drawled from the other side of the circle. "Too many ex-wives were buying bed bugs and releasing them in their ex-husbands' beds while he and that floozie he took up with were out for the day?"

Several of us chuckled. It might have only been the wind, but I could swear I heard "well, shoot" muttered from more than one place around the room. "So, folks," I said, "what shall we do? Take up a collection? What did you say, Lauren. four hundred dollars?"

"Ah, yes. Four hundred dollars for twelve doses successfully delivered."

I removed my lucky Giants baseball cap, popped two twenties into it and passed it to Helen, who started digging in her purse.

Nina eyed the hat, headed her way. "Um, Lauren, do you know how they deliver the medication? I mean, does it hurt the pigs?"

"Ah, as I understand it, they first tranquilize the animal. Then they give it a quick check up, vaccinate it against ... " Lauren stopped and read from her notes, "leptospirosis, inject it with the fertility inhibitor, and tag its ear."

"Oh no, not vaccines, too." Jessica muttered.

Lauren looked up. "Ah, that's so your children don't get leptospirosis from the pigs." Jessica buried her face in her hands.

I don't actually know what leptospirosis is, but it does not sound like something I want anyone to get. I think that's one of those horrid-sounding diseases my dogs get vaccinated against.

"Anyway," Lauren continued, "they stay with the animal until it can walk away on its own."

"Both males and females?" Helen asked.

"Ah, good question," Lauren said. "I'll ask when I call."

My hat continued on its journey. When it came back to me it contained two hundred and fifty seven dollars and twenty two cents, plus two IOUs one penned on a napkin and the other on the torn side of a styrofoam cup. Some joker had also dropped in the cap from a beer bottle. Considering the money we might collect from those not attending the meeting, I gave Lauren a thumbs up, and Graciela called for us to adjourn.

CHAPTER FIFTEEN

Out on the porch in the warm evening, Helen remarked how it was too bad the people who owned the McMansion wouldn't be contributing their share toward the control of the wild boar population. "If they really are mobsters, they'd have a lot of spare change to contribute, too," she added.

"So what is the story with that, 'Stel'? We haven't seen much of you or that Muñoz the last day or so. Did you figure out who killed that boy? Was it the mobsters, like we thought?"

I explained how Muñoz had spent the day interviewing other possible persons of interest, including the kids who had found the dinghy, but since we weren't clear about their connection with the body on the beach, that line of conversation fizzled out. "About the only thing we've learned is that the kids he went to school with don't seem to like Chip much. If the body is Chip."

"Mr. Muñoz does think those other children had something to do with that poor boy, then?" Freda asked.

"Yeah, kids these days." Helen shook her head, despairing of the younger generation. "What's with all this bullying you hear about?"

Freda's head bobbed in agreement. "Yes, and they knew where the little boat was, isn't that right, Estela? They must have been the ones who took it out. What did that little boat have to do with that poor boy?"

"Good question," I said. "We don't know there really is a connection, but if there is, what could it be?"

"I don't want to think other children had anything to do with what happened to that boy," Nina said. "It might have been an accident. You know, with the drugs? What did you call them, roofies? Possibly the boy took too many and, well, you know, passed away. The children got scared and tried to hide his body."

"Maybe," I said. "That might explain the amateurish way the body was tied with rope and the weight that fell off. And that might be the connection between the dinghy and the body."

We stood on the porch chatting, and absently watching two of Arroyo Loco's resident teenagers playing catch with a football in front. Actually, they were playing two games, the first being catch with the football, and the second being the game of chicken as the occasional automobile peeled off the highway and headed up the road at a reckless rate of speed. The kids could as easily and more safely been playing in the vacant lot designated as our park, but that lot is bordered on its far side by a drop off into a steep and treacherous canyon. Any ball that bounces out of control there is gone for good.

I hesitate to call an idea that should have occurred to me days ago a bright idea, but while watching the kids, it did at least slowly dawn on me that I might ask them if they knew anything about Chip. We live in a rural area and all the teenagers in this part of the county go to the same high school over in Morro Bay. Possibly our kids might know the kids in Cayucos, too.

About that time, Grant rolled up in his LeSabre. Apparently, he had walked home and was returning to offer Helen and the rest of us rides up the hill to our homes. I passed on the offer and waved goodbye.

"Hey, Randy and DeVon." I motioned the teenagers over.

"'Sup?" Randy said, taking a seat on a step. DeVon continued to stand, tossing the football from hand to hand.

I got right to the point, so as not to distract them too long from their game. "Do you guys know these kids who live at the top of the hill? You know, in the big house?" DeVon gave Randy an inscrutable look, and Randy developed a sudden interest in a splinter on the wooden step. I tried again. "Don't you guys go to school with them?" I don't know DeVon as well, but it was unlike Randy to be reluctant to talk to me. "Randy? What's going on?"

He shook his head, still picking at the splinter. "It'd be better if you'd jus' let that one drop," he finally said.

"What does that mean? You heard we found the boy, Chip, dead, right?"

"Yeah, we heard that." The boys cut glances at each other again. I could read between those lines. Not-so-subtle communication about how much they should say. Randy's shoulders lifted in a shrug.

"Look, Estela, that Chip and his supposed sister, they're not kids. Nobody knows what the deal is, but I'm just sayin' you shouldn't get too involved in questioning those folks."

"You mean because of their connection with the mob guys? Their parents, right?"

DeVon huffed and looked away.

"Okay," I said. "So the Malakovs are not Chip and Sissy's parents?"

Randy was getting frustrated with my questions. "Chip is ...
was ... not a kid. And if you want ... wanted ... drugs, any kind
of drugs you want, if you're into that, Chip was the guy to see.
A total creep. I'm just saying, stay away from that." He lowered
his brow at me, as though giving me a command.

"I heard he can get you a fake id, too," DeVon added. "For
really cheap. Plus, what he does to the girls."

"Yeah," Randy agreed.

"What?" I could guess, but if I was going to pass this
information along to Muñoz I wanted to be clear about what
they were saying.

"We heard Chip uses drugs on the girls, then, you know ... "
Randy said.

"Takes advantage of them?" Both boys nodded, looking
away.

"You do know, when a boy does that, it's called rape, right?
Even if the girl is so drugged she doesn't resist, it's still assault."

"Not in California it's not," Randy said.

"What?"

"If the girl is unconscious, having sex on her isn't a felony
in California."

I took hold of Randy's arm and tried not to become
hysterical. "What?"

"That's just the law."

"Yeah," DeVon added, "unless you hit her."

"How on earth did that become the law? I don't remember
hearing anything about that!" The boys both raised their
eyebrows and started to step back. "I'm calling my state senator
in the morning. This is outrageous!" Especially disturbing, I
thought, that teenage boys knew that, but I didn't.

"We didn't ever do it," DeVon said in a defensive tone.

153

"Well, good, and I hope you stop any guy who tries anything like that." They nodded again. "Did either of you ever report these rumors about Chip to anyone, maybe someone at the school, or a cop?"

"We never saw him do it," DeVon said. "We just heard from some of the girls."

"The girls?" I asked. "You how Chip ended up. Do either of you think the girls might have had something to do with that?"

"We don't know," Randy said, standing.

"We don't know about that," DeVon echoed.

They both made long, convincing eye contact with me. If either of them had said more than that, added the word honestly, or said they didn't know anything at all, I would have had doubts, but knowing them as I did, I was assured they really did not know any more than what they'd told me.

The sun had long since slipped below the hills surrounding our canyon. Even though we were approaching the longest day of the year, the summer solstice, it was late enough that darkness had fully fallen. Our new sidewalks and streetlights made the walk home less intimidating than in the past. Just the same, there were those boar out there. After we thought we might have heard guttural grunting in the darkness to our left, the boys took up positions on either side of me, and we all walked briskly uphill.

Muñoz had chocolate supermarket donuts and break room coffee available in a small conference room when I arrived Tuesday morning at the sheriff's substation. We had arrangements to meet with three of the five teenagers who admitted to being among the group that had known Chip. Hoping the interviews would be productive, and knowing they might take up most of the morning, I had dropped both dogs off at the sheep ranch before my arrival at the substation.

Cameras in two corners filmed the interview, making note-taking unnecessary. All the same, Muñoz had equipped himself with a pad of paper and a pencil. I was less well-prepared.

Our first interviewee, Kevin, arrived with his mother right on time. We settled in at the table while Kevin's mother busied herself chatting with the deputy on duty out at the front desk. I managed to resist the less-than-quality donuts, but Kevin dug right in. Unfortunately, he had little to add to his previous interview. He failed to be impressed with the presence of a psychologist, which I found surprising. Many people assume psychologists are also psychics, and can read minds.

He did admit to being present on the cabin cruiser for a "get-together," sometime in the past. He wasn't sure if he'd been there two, or possibly three weeks prior, and said he would not describe the event as a party. That much was at least more than Muñoz had gotten out of him previously. Kevin also could not remember who else might have been present on that occasion.

The detective's brow lowered in frustration, and he slapped a plastic bag on the table, the white capsule inside. "Care to explain this?"

Kevin blanched. "What is that?"

"Your mother found it in your pocket. Why don't you tell us what it is?"

"I don't know."

We'd heard that answer too many times before. Muñoz shifted his jaw and gave Kevin an angry stare.

"I swear, I don't know. Chip gave it to me, that night on the boat. He told me to put it in Madison's beer, but Madison was hanging out on the bow? Madison was upset about something with Chip, and she stayed up there with the other girl, so I just put the pill in my pocket and forgot about it." Kevin could not tell us if Chip had more of the capsules, and couldn't remember if Chip had been alone with Madison at other parties. He also swore he had no idea why Chip had fallen asleep at the party that night on the cabin-cruiser.

Oops. A long silence fell over the interview room while each of us digested the information Kevin had spilled in his rush to convince us he knew nothing.

"Tell you what," Muñoz said, "let's start over again. You were present at a party on the cabin-cruiser about two weeks ago, is that correct?"

Kevin's face crumpled and his shoulders dropped for a moment. He looked up and nodded.

"I need you to speak, Kevin, so your voice will be recorded on the tape."

"Yes, I was there."

"And who else was there?"

"I don't remember."

Muñoz's jaw shifted again and I actually heard his teeth grind. Detective Muñoz is a big man, but he has a gentle soul. I hated to see him get angry. On the other hand, this situation would frustrate anyone. Might be time for the professional psychologist to step in.

"Okay, Kevin," I said. "Let's see here. You've already said that Chip was there, right?"

He looked miserable, but realized he'd already given that information up. "Yes."

"Good. And you've already said that Madison was there with another girl."

"Yes, Jennifer," he said, naming another of the kids who had been in Kevin's driveway.

156

"So there were three girls there, Madison, Jennifer, and Ashley?" I took a flyer and added Ashley, since she was with the group in the the driveway, and was, in fact, waiting to be interviewed next.

"Yes."

"And three boys, Chip, you, and ... that other guy? The guy with the long hair? Brown?" I vaguely remembered a kid matching that description from my encounter with the group in Kevin's driveway.

"David," Muñoz said.

"Is that right, Kevin?" I asked. "Was anyone else at that party?"

"I don't remember."

I looked at Muñoz. Guess we'd played out that line of inquiry. Still, we had learned a lot more than we'd known when we started. The detective thanked Kevin and dismissed him. He leaned over his notepad, trying to get everything on paper before we started the next interview.

Ashley arrived with an angry-looking father, tears already streaming down her cheeks. The father got caught up in conversation with another parent also in the waiting area and waved goodbye to his daughter.

Once in the interview room, Ashley immediately admitted to being present on the boat with the same four other kids we'd found in Kevin's driveway last week, plus Chip.

"It was a week ago Thursday," she said, "the last time."

She hiccuped, and with some gentle encouragement from me, continued. "Chip invited us. It was his boat. Or his family's. He drove us out there in one of those black cars. and he brought the beer? I don't really like beer? I drank it though, because Chip was acting like he was starting to like me? Ashley was using that annoying up-speak voice where every sentence

157

ends with a questioning tone. I've noticed lately that up-speak has become quite popular among young people, particularly on public radio. I can handle about three sentences of up-speak. Then I just want to grab the speaker by the shoulders and shake him or her. Just for pity's sake, make a declarative statement. Up-speak is especially annoying when the speaker is making a statement about which no one else could possibly know, as Ashley was doing this morning.

"I drank the beer because I wanted Chip to like me?"

See what I mean? Up-speak is exhausting for the listener. It demands constant attention, nodding and responding. Only Ashley could know why she drank the beer, but she made it sound like we should be able to tell her why she did it.

"Did you like Chip?" I said.

She gave me a confused look. Could have meant anything from "of course I liked him" to "why would I like him?" Interpreting meaning from facial expressions has always been a weak point for the psychotherapist in me. Maybe she was only wondering why I was asking about Chip in the present tense.

"Or, I mean, did you like Chip? And what about Sissy? Are you friends with Sissy, too?"

Ashley shrugged, non-committal. "She's okay. She's old, though. They're both too old for high school. Like, Sissy has these crinkles by her eyes? She has to be nineteen, at least. They said they moved around a lot? We just figured they missed out on a year or two of school for whatever reason. We didn't want to ask?"

"And was Sissy at the party, too" I said, increasingly curious about the Odam's alleged children.

"No, no. She doesn't hang out much with Chip. We don't know why. Seems like she doesn't like him."

"Okay," Muñoz jumped in, "Let's get back to that night on the cabin-cruiser. You were drinking beer because you wanted Chip to like you. Then what happened?"

"Nothing happened. It was just, we were there. Last month, Chip was all over Madison? Now she doesn't like him any more, and he's being nice to me ... or he was ... " She dissolved in sobs again.

I couldn't decide if Ashley had gone off on a tangent of grief, or if she was giving us useful information. I pressed for something more concrete.

"So, you, Jennifer, and Madison, were at the party?"

Ashley narrowed her eyes, suspicion reflected in her expression. "Yes ... ?"

"And Chip, Kevin, and David?"

She spoke slowly again, clearly trying to figure out what I was up to. "First of all, you couldn't really call Chip a boy. He had to be at least twenty-one. You know, because he buys us beer?"

I nodded, not agreeing or disagreeing. After all, according to DeVon, the kids could buy fake ids from Chip, so possibly Chip had supplied himself with a fake id for the purpose of buying alcohol. Anyway, how could a twenty-one year old have convinced anyone he was of high school age?

What else did we need to know? According to Bob, the waiter, Chip was stumbling around alone late on the night of the party.

Muñoz beat me to the punch. "What time did you leave the boat that night, Ashley?" He tapped at the notebook with his stubby pencil.

"We had to leave early. Friday, that was the last day of school? Us girls, we had to be home by eleven? I mean, the boys were supposed to be home, too, but I guess they didn't

159

care. Anyway, we didn't want to get in trouble, and Chip was like, he was like drunk? Or something?" She turned wide open eyes on us at that point, the kind of expression that people seem to think makes them look innocent. My take was, that face said "guilty" all over it. I fired a look at Muñoz, but he appeared to be buying the virtuous act.

"Anyway," she went on, "he couldn't drive, and he wouldn't give us the keys? David tried to get him to give us the keys, but he wouldn't. He even hit David. Well, he didn't mean to. Chip swung his arm, like, and knocked David down? So we couldn't get the keys. We couldn't even get out the gate to the pier. So Kevin said we should take the dinghy and motor up to Cayucos, and that's what we did. Chip was alive when we left, I swear. David just told him, like, you take a nap and we'll be back?" Ashley shrugged and raised her hands, palm upwards. Really, her expression said, what could she possibly have had to do with a body found days later?

By the time Ashley had sobbed her way through the rest of her story, the interview had gone on far longer than anticipated. The next boy, David, had been cooling his heels in the front office for half an hour. Muñoz led Ashley to a rear exit, and we spent a few minutes strategizing our next interview.

According to Ashley's story, all five teenagers had ridden the dinghy out of the bay to the ocean side of Morro Rock where they nearly capsized in the waves. They stuck close to shore after that, and were able to safely off-load onto the beach in Cayucos. They were tempted to leave the dinghy there, but Kevin and David were concerned about returning it. They figured when they got back, they'd rouse Chip. He would probably have sobered up by then and they would have him drive them home. Anyway, they wanted to make sure Chip was

160

okay. Ashley thought it was odd the boys were so concerned about Chip, since no one liked him much. Nevertheless, the two boys puttered off into the night, leaving the girls on the beach close to their homes.

Muñoz and I decided to use the interview with David to get new information, rather than merely corroborating what we'd already learned. When I went to fetch David, he was sitting alone in one of the naugahyde and chrome chairs.

"I'm sorry," I said, trying to be welcoming in spite of the reason for our meeting. "Did your mom get tired of waiting?"

I wasn't sure David was going to answer me as he unfolded his long thin body from the chair. "Nah," he finally said. "She rode into work with Ashley's dad. Left me the car."

Muñoz pasted on his stern face as David slouched in and took up a relaxed pose in our plastic chair. I went for my concerned psychotherapist look, a warm smile, soft eyes, and a slightly furrowed brow. David glanced at me, and his eyebrows went up and down. I may have overdone the sympathetic expression, or maybe he wasn't feeling the need.

I started with some non-threatening questions, asked him if he'd had a good time at the party, that sort of thing. At first he didn't have much to add to what we already knew, having been remarkably unobservant on the night in question. About the only piece he was able to add to the puzzle was a story about how Chip had been found in a dumpster, "the yucky one, behind the cafeteria," a couple of weeks before. The rumor was, he'd been left in there by a bunch of girls. The handle of a pink hairbrush was jammed into the latch to trap Chip inside.

"Guess no one liked Chip," I said. "We've heard stories from other kids, too. Hoping you can fill in some blanks." He cocked his head at me, a good sign, so I launched into more difficult topics.

CHAPTER SIXTEEN

The interview with David had started slowly, and I tried to pick up the pace.

"Did you and Kevin get back to the cabin-cruiser okay?" I said. My question apparently startled David because his forehead crinkled. After a half a second, his expression cleared. I may have accidentally given him an alternative explanation for what happened that night. Maybe he and Kevin simply ditched the dinghy and had never seen Chip again.

I plowed ahead. "And how was Chip doing when you got there? We have a witness who says Chip was alive after you left." Muñoz shot me an angry glare. I had just given David another way out. Maybe Chip wasn't even there when the boys returned. Might be a good idea for me to shut-up for a while.

"Look, David," Muñoz said, "we know Chip had roofies in his system when he died. Some alcohol, and an overdose of rohypnol. He wouldn't have done that to himself. We know you were there, so, David, we just want you to tell us, how did that happen?"

Muñoz's question sounded like an accusation to me. David had the same reaction.

He froze, his long arms folded across his chest. His lips tightened. It didn't look to me like we were going to get anything at all out of David. He was done talking. His eyes
162

narrowed, focused on the blank wall. Something about the way his whole body tensed made me wonder, and the corners of his eyes glistened. He was on the verge of tears. Facial expressions may confuse me, but body language speaks volumes, and David's posture screamed guilt.

A face unexpectedly appearing in the salt-encrusted window on the side wall startled all of us. Ashley cupped her hands around her eyes, and she focused on David. He rose and stepped to the door.

"Gotta go," he said, as though this interview with Detective Muñoz was a mere formality, and something he could walk out on any time he felt like it. And actually, Muñoz informed me after David left, it was. In spite of our official interview room, and Muñoz with his badge clipped in full view on his dress shirt, these teenagers were not under arrest, and under no real obligation to talk to us. Yet.

"Well, phooey," I said. "Those kids really didn't like Chip. We have to find a way to make them talk."

"At least the girls don't like Chip."

"You're right about that. Do you think they didn't like him enough to kill him?"

Muñoz only looked at me, saying nothing. Then he cocked one eyebrow in skepticism.

"What?" I said. "You think the girls couldn't have killed Chip?"

He shook his head. "Hard to imagine, don't you think?"

"Why? Because they're girls? Why is it so hard to believe the girls might have killed Chip? Especially given what Chip was doing to them. Are you one of those guys who think girls and women are going to put up with that kind of treatment forever, in silence, without ever fighting back? Maybe those girls had just had enough."

163

The detective looked at me, and shook his head again. "No, I'm not one of those guys. I'm only thinking, if girls and women start exacting retribution ... if that happens, there's going to be one heck of a lot more crime to investigate. That's all."

"True enough. When you think, ninety-eight percent of all violent crime is committed by men, and most of that is committed against women, if women start fighting back, egads! The violent crime rate could double overnight."

"I'll tell you one thing I think is obvious," he said. "Whether they killed him or not, those kids had something to do with getting that rohypnol into Chip, that's what I think."

For at least a full minute, we sat in glum silence.

"So, what did we learn?" I said.

"A fair amount we didn't already know. Not anything about how Chip died."

He paused, tapping his pencil again.

"Here are my impressions," I said. "At least among the boys, Kevin is the leader of this group. David is also strong-willed, with a mind of his own, although Ashley does exert considerable control over him." Across the table, Muñoz's eyes were beginning to glaze over. I fast-forwarded to what he might consider the important part.

"We also learned that this group of teenagers were present on the Poddelka with Chip very close to the time he likely died. All of the kids knew Chip was, let's say, incapacitated, that night on the boat. And at least Kevin knew drugs were present. Kevin is not telling us everything he knows. We need to talk to him again, maybe in a slightly more intimidating environment. Could that be arranged?"

"Possibly ...."

164

"Let's think about a timeline here. Chip was alive, although not in great shape when the five kids took the dinghy and left him at roughly around half past ten."

"Yeah. And they had already left when Chip fell in the water and Bob fished him out."

"Yes. Bob saw Chip still alive after the kids left, at about eleven, so unless they'd slipped him something long-acting the medical examiner can't find, the kids didn't kill Chip."

"But Kevin and David came back, more than an hour later. Was Chip still alive when they got back? Could they have killed him then?"

"Or, was Chip even there when they got back? Because remember, Bob called the parents. Someone could have picked Chip up, so that by the time Kevin and David got back, Chip might have already been gone."

"Why wouldn't they just tell us that, then?"

"Good point."

"And remember, Bob only left a message on the answering machine. We don't know if anyone got the message."

"Okay," Muñoz said, "so we need to know if Kevin and David made it back to the cabin-cruiser, if Chip was there when they got there, and if he was, was he still alive. Oh, hang on." He abruptly left the room, returning seconds later with several official-looking pages. "This is the evidence recovery report from the dinghy. They found prints and trace evidence from several individuals, including the three kids who were just here, and the other two as well."

"So that's corroboration for their story," I said, "that they were on the dinghy, although it doesn't tell us when they were on it. Here's the thing, though. If Chip's body was dumped into the ocean, and we think it was, and it wasn't dumped off the cabin-cruiser, which it probably wasn't because someone would have seen a cruiser that size motoring out of the marina and through the bay at that time of night."

"And you think the body had to have been dumped off the dinghy?"

"Well, that body could have been dumped off any boat, of course. It's just that now we have this dinghy puttering around, and well, it seems likely there was a connection there. That's what I'm thinking. My friend Evan says the body had to have been dumped somewhere north of where it was found, and was pushed to the beach by the current. Can the evidence recovery people find anything indicating that not just the kids, but Chip also was on the dinghy? Or someone else entirely? You know, like the boys brought the dinghy back, and then later, someone else took it and dumped the body?"

"If that happened, how did the boys get home?"

"Oh. Yes, good point. Is Chip's car still in the parking lot at the marina?"

"No. Or at least there are no cars that have been sitting there all this time. City police would have had any vehicle towed by now. It's illegal to park there all night without a permit."

"And they didn't tow anything that night?"

"Not that I know of. I'll check again, but no."

"So, then where is Chip's car? Did the boys take it and abandon it somewhere else?"

"Okay, okay. I'll look into it. There are usually two black cars up at the big house. I don't know anything about this Chip having his own car, but I'll look into it."

"Yes, because think about it. According to the kids, Chip drove them all out to the marina in his car. So regardless of what happened to Chip and his body, where is his car?"

166

Muñoz shook his head slowly back and forth like a confused buffalo. Probably it was time for me to shut-up with the insights.

"Begins to sound like possibly Kevin and David had something to do with Chip's death, or at least getting rid of the body," Muñoz said.

"Yes, and that's if you believe Ashley's story about the girls being dropped off before Kevin and David took the dinghy back. And if they took the dinghy back, how in the heck did it end up on the beach north of Cayucos?"

Muñoz and I both were talking and thinking at the same time.

"What if the boys returned to the cabin-cruiser, found Chip still unable to drive, and took the dinghy back up to Cayucos to get home?"

"And hid the dinghy in that cove? Why would they hide it?" I said.

"Technically, they did steal it. Trying to cover up the theft?"

"Maybe. How does that explain finding Chip's body on the beach four days later?"

Muñoz shook his head. "It doesn't. We need more information. I'd need a warrant to arrest them, but I can bring in and detain Kevin and David under probable cause. They might talk if I mention the word arrest."

"And Ashley."

"Why Ashley?"

"I just think Ashley knows something."

"I don't think there's grounds to arrest Ashley."

I scowled "Well, phooey. Then we need to find another way to talk to her.

Even though I'd only eaten two, or maybe three of them, the donuts formed a heavy wad in my stomach. This did not prevent me from noticing that it was well past lunch time when we finished the interviews. Sometimes I think I tend to eat when it's time to eat, and not necessarily when I'm hungry. I suggested to Muñoz that we go out in search of lunch, preferably something light. His phone buzzed as we were finishing big salads at the counter in the natural foods grocery.

He managed to get through the entire call without uttering one complete word except his last name. After the long series of "uh-huhs, hmms," and "huhs," he disconnected. "Dr. Rajavi wants to talk," he told me. "You got time?"

My dogs were probably having a much better day at the sheep ranch than they would if I took them home and made them watch me relax, so I agreed to go along to hear what was on the doctor's mind.

As we sat down in the meeting room, Dr. Rajavi handed Muñoz a copy of the official autopsy report and made him sign for it. He slid it across the table to me, and I perused it studiously. It was mostly medical terms and technical anatomical jargon, peppered here and there with disturbing descriptions of decay and putrefaction. I slid it back, nodding as though I had been sufficiently elucidated.

"That isn't what I wanted to talk to you about," the doctor said. Although Muñoz and I both looked interested, neither of us managed so much as a grunt. She waited a moment, then went on. "It was the manner of death that had me stumped."

I nodded, and she took that as encouragement. "As you know, the deceased had a small amount of sea water in his lungs. Not enough to cause drowning. Stomach contents also included a small amount of alcohol, possibly as much as two beers, and a few chewed nuts."

168

I dropped my forehead into my hands for a moment. Why did she have to put it like that? Images of stomach contents made my head swirl. Why couldn't she just say he drank and ate those things? That way I could picture him at the party enjoying himself. She glanced my way, then continued.

"Again, no reason to think those had any bearing on his subsequent death. The amount of rohypnol in his blood stream was high enough to have caused dizziness, sleepiness, even semi-consciousness in a person of that size, but again, without some other cause, that would not have resulted in death. And remember, there are no signs of trauma on the body."

Muñoz stared at the doctor somberly. From all outward appearances, he was attending to what she said, but I knew him well enough to be able to guess with certainty that inside his head he was urging her to hurry up and get to the point. I'm not sure how he was able to transmit this thought without moving a muscle, but the doctor looked at him, then sped up her narrative.

"Determining the level of oxygen in the blood is very difficult this long after death, and especially after the body has been submerged in sea water for three to four days. Nevertheless, I did see some signs there may have been a depletion of oxygen in the blood."

"And that would cause death," Muñoz said. His tone did not indicate a question.

Dr. Rajavi was nodding. "Blood oxygen can be depleted in a variety of ways. A pulmonary embolism, for example, can cut off oxygenation to the blood. But there was no evidence of an embolism in this young man. Intentional or accidental choking can also result in lowered oxygen in the blood."

I pictured a teenager or two wringing Chip's neck. No wonder they were acting guilty. The doctor continued.

"If the manner of this death had been accidental choking, I would almost certainly have found signs of that during autopsy. A piece of food lodged in the trachea, for example."

By this time, I was gazing at the wall, trying not to picture anything. I had to give this forensic pathologist credit for her thoroughness.

"When choking is intentional, which is indeed not uncommon among young people ...."

Muñoz and I glanced at each other, both sadly aware that choking to unconsciousness is not an uncommon sexual practice among young people.

I missed the next few sentences while I tried not to picture that scene.

"Anyway," she went on, "if this young man died as a result of another person pressing their hands around his throat, or even using an object to cause strangulation, I would be seeing trauma on the neck, and as I said earlier, there are no such signs."

Muñoz was tapping an invisible pencil against the table, and even I was getting a bit impatient. Hanging out at the forensic pathologist's office listening to her ramble on about various causes of death was giving me a stomachache. Or maybe it was those donuts.

"And, so?" Muñoz said. Tap, tap, tap. Any minute, his knee was going to start that jiggling thing it does now and then.

"So, smothering can also deplete blood oxygen enough to cause death. With a young man such as the deceased, smothering is difficult due to his ability to fight off an attacker, but remember, this young man was likely in a semiconscious state due to the effects of the roofies he had consumed or been fed. His ability to fight off an attacker would have been severely compromised by the large amount of rohypnol in his blood."

"So, you're saying he was smothered? Like with a pillow or something?" I said. She was right. It was hard to imagine Chip not fighting off someone trying to smother him with a pillow.

"Yes, that does appear to be the likely cause of death," she said. "Smothering sometimes leaves signs of trauma, but not always. In any case, I decided to look for other signs that the deceased may have been smothered."

"And those other signs would be?" Muñoz said.

Here she launched into a description of what she did to the body to discover those other signs. Let me spare the details and cut to the chase by simply saying she did indeed find cotton fibers inside the throat and lungs of the deceased, indicating that, although the alcohol, rohypnol, and near-drowning had been contributing factors, Chip's final cause of death was that he had been smothered with something made of cotton. Now it would be up to us to find the physical evidence.

Muñoz scrunched his brow into the most puzzled frown I'd ever seen on him. "Cotton, like a pillow. Wouldn't a woman be more likely than a man to use a pillow as a murder weapon?"

I had no idea. Wondered why he would make that assumption, unless it was because making beds was women's work.

"Knowing that would be your department, detective," Dr. Rajavi said.

We had barely absorbed that piece of information when she added, "Oh, and I have one other thing for you, if you'll wait one second." She left the room and quickly returned, clutching another piece of paper.

"The sheriff's office sent over the results of that Rapid DNA test they ran, I guess on a cloth napkin?"

Muñoz and I both nodded. I suppressed a desire to whisper "I told you so," to him.

"They did find DNA from two individuals on the napkin, allegedly the parents of the deceased? I tried to match those up with the sample I collected from the deceased, but there was no match."

"No match at all?" Muñoz said.

"Meaning neither of those people was related to Chip?" I said.

"Not biologically related, no."

"So, Chip is not their son at all?" Muñoz said.

"Not biologically," the doctor confirmed. "He might be adopted, or related by marriage. A step-son, for example."

"But he's not biologically related to either the mother or the father," I said, "so unlikely a step-son."

"Oh, yes. You are right. Not biologically related to either of those individuals."

That gave us something to think about. Muñoz and I strolled to the parking lot, both lost in thought. It felt like the universe had shifted, as though someone had turned the puzzle ninety degrees and it didn't even look like the same puzzle any longer.

"Seems like, the more we learn, the more questions we have."

Muñoz agreed with a nod.

"Like, does the pathologist still have the rope and sheet-thing the body was wrapped in? Would there be DNA or some other kind of evidence on that thing that would indicate who wrapped the body?"

The detective sighed, pulled out his notebook, and started jotting down notes.

"I guess it's kind of a no-brainer that those birth certificates are counterfeit. I mean, that's what the guy does. He's a counterfeiter. But who is Chip if he's not their son?"

"Yeah, and, who is this Sissy person?"

"Good point. And where is she? We don't have any DNA, or fingerprints from her. If we can't find her, we might never know who she is. Did your techs find any unidentified prints when they dusted the house?"

"Hang on, let me write that down. We might be able to match her prints up if she's in the system. Any other questions?"

"Sure would be nice if we could track down Mr. and Mrs. Odam or Malakov or whoever they are and just ask them." I gazed through the windshield for a bit. Seemed like, adding more pieces to the puzzle would make it easier to put some of them together, but instead, the additional pieces only added to the confusion.

"You know," I said, "a simple answer is that Kevin and David found Chip passed out when they made it back to the Poddelka, smothered him, then dumped the body."

"Or Bob smothered him."

"Another simple answer. Except then how did the body get dumped? We need to ask Bob if anyone else saw him leave at eleven, like he said he did."

Muñoz made another note. "You mean like, Chip is such a lousy tipper Bob gets mad enough to smother him?"

I could hear the smirk in his voice. "Okay, well I guess we are getting a little punchy. The point is, between Bob and the kids, we already have some fairly viable suspects. Maybe we don't need to bring anyone else into this."

"True. Only ...."

I waited.

"Remember, we're dealing with dangerous mobsters. If a murder was committed, what are the odds it was done by a group of previously innocent kids, versus a bunch of convicted and violent mobsters?"

Muñoz had a point. I asked him to take me back to my car. I wanted to pick up my dogs and spend some quality time at the beach contemplating this problem.

CHAPTER SEVENTEEN

I contemplated so deeply as I walked the beach, that when I looked up, the dogs and I were nearly parallel to Evan's house. The glass door on his deck opened and Jax bounded out, shaking his nap off in a blonde retriever cloud of fur. From the doorway, Evan lifted a wine bottle in my direction, but I waved off the offer. Later, I would need to navigate the winding road to Arroyo Loco, a challenging enough trip without alcohol-induced impairment.

Our dogs were well into their usual romp when Evan joined me on the beach. Although I was interested in what Evan might know about Chip, Sissy, and the rest of the kids, and very curious about why he had been digging in his side yard the other day, I kept our conversation to the usual banter about dog issues, at least at first.

Shiner brought me a rotting tennis ball he had unearthed from under something. He dropped it at my feet and gazed up at me, quivering in hopes I would throw it. Even in good condition, tennis balls are not great toys for dogs. I scooped this one up in a clean poop bag, popped it in my fanny pack and extracted our rubber ball. With sadness, I noted that I had been so deep in thought that I'd left our Chuckit throwing device in the car.

I personally do not think my throwing skills are inadequate, but even I had to admit, my toss was disappointingly short. Shiner loves it when the ball sails so far and so fast he has to run full out, his legs stretching to their limit as he gallops after the ball. When he brought it back, I handed the ball to Evan to see what he could do with it. All three dogs racing down the beach together was a beautiful sight, the kind of thing that feeds my soul. We played that way until Scout, being the older dog, had given up, and even Jax plopped into the sand, panting. Shiner, of course, would have gone on chasing the ball endlessly. Another good thing about a rubber ball is, one swipe with a tissue, and it's dry enough to zip into the fanny pack.

"Any progress on that investigation?" Evan asked, drying his hands on the seat of his pants.

"Some. More questions than answers, I'm afraid. Turns out there was a group of kids, high school kids, partying with Chip earlier on the night he died. Do you know any of the kids who hung out with Chip?"

"Probably. I know most of the students there. It's not a large school. That's why I suggested you talk to some of the other kids. Did you do that?"

"Yes, a few. The ones who partied with Chip anyway. We heard a rumor." Knowing how to best word my question slowed me down. "Anyway, something about Chip and the girls at school?"

"Chip and the date-rape rumors, you mean?"

"Yes. What do you know about that?"

"Not a lot. I do know those two caused trouble from the moment they showed up. And nobody believes they're really eighteen and sixteen."

"What kind of trouble? I mean, other than drugging the girls, and I don't mean to imply that's not enough right there."

176

Evan paused, gazing into the distance. "Has your detective talked to the city police?"

I indicated confusion, and Evan continued.

"This so-called Chip and Sissy were running this scam on weekends in town, you know, down by the mission? They were targeting tourists. Nearly got caught a couple times. They worked it on the university campus, and even once at the high school."

Not being all that familiar with your average criminal scam operation, I was at a loss as to what Even was talking about. I gave him another confused look.

"Okay, well, here's how it works. Chip carries a beautifully tailored expensive-looking leather jacket and approaches a likely looking target. This is a really nice jacket, in the range of a couple thousand to buy. Chip tells the target a sob story about how he really needs money. Different story every time. Dying grandmother, hungry family, vet bills to save his beloved dog, whatever. Asks the guy to please buy the jacket off him for an incredible price, and something the guy might even have on him in cash. A hundred, two hundred. This is for a two-, three-thousand dollar jacket. Chump can't resist, gives Chip the money, puts on the pricey jacket."

So far, I wasn't seeing where this was going. I couldn't understand how this would make any money for Chip and Sissy. I waited, and Evan continued.

"Then, fifteen minutes or so later, Sissy comes running up to the target. 'Oh, no!' she says, 'That's my jacket!' She turns on the waterworks with a story about how her parents gave her the jacket. They'll kill her if she loses it. Says she put it down for two seconds, and some guy grabbed it and ran. 'You have to give it back to me,' she yells. To cap off her story, she shows the guy her name sewn into the jacket and her id. Fake, of course.

177

If the target seems even a trifle doubtful, and the tears aren't working, Sissy suggests calling the cops, since the target is in possession of stolen property. He gives in, gives her the jacket, and she's gone."

"With the jacket."

"And Chip still has the one or two hundred in cash. They can run the scam multiple times, collecting money every time."

"Oh, man." I was at a loss for words. "Who thinks up these things?"

"I'm just saying, I don't think anyone is going to miss Chip or Sissy too much, especially not the other students."

I nodded while Evan gazed out over the ocean again. He shrugged. "A week ago Friday was the last day of classes. The halls are quiet now. Word has it, the kids took care of the problem themselves."

I stopped breathing for a moment. More often than we tend to realize, crimes are solved by the perpetrator admitting guilt, sometimes out of remorse, or maybe more often out of boastful pride. "What do you mean, 'word has it?' Do you mean someone is claiming credit for killing Chip?"

"I'm only repeating what I heard in the faculty lunchroom earlier this week. Guy in chemistry pointed out Chip is gone. Sissy is gone. He said, the word is, the kids took care of them."

"Nothing more specific than that? And Sissy, too? She's missing, you know? Maybe we just haven't found her body yet?" Evan raised his hands in a gesture of surrender. Guess the guy was out of information. We had drifted closer to his steps by then. I cut a quick glance in the direction of his side yard, hoping to see what he had been digging over there the other day, but couldn't see around the deck.

All three dogs' tongues were hanging out at near record lengths, so we went on up and Evan filled and refilled a big

178

ceramic dish with fresh water. The dogs took turns happily slobbering water all over the deck and each other. This gave me the opportunity to lean over the railing and take a good gander at that side yard. Sure enough, the sandy dirt there had been dug up in a rectangle about six feet long. A rusting garden spade leaned against the wall of the house.

Dare I ask Evan what he'd buried there? He came to lean casually next to me. At least, it seemed to me he was remarkably casual about leaning there. I turned and tried to gauge how long it would take my dogs and me to fly across the deck and down the steps, should we need to make a fast getaway. It was far enough that, if Evan wanted to stop me, we'd never make it.

I asked for a glass of water, then took the opportunity while he was inside getting it to call my dogs off the deck. I stood at the top of the steps.

"Thanks," I said when he brought me the water. I drank it. "I really need to get going." I started to back down the steps.

"Yes, I need to get back to my garden," he said. "If we don't have too much fog this summer, I should be able to get some tomatoes going on that south side of the house."

"Oh, yes, a garden. Yes, of course." I kept going, and waved goodbye. A garden. Hmph. I doubted it. Still, which made more sense, Evan planting a garden, or Evan killing a young woman and burying her body in a shallow grave next to his house where Jax would likely dig it up? Maybe I was spending too much time investigating crime.

I made the turn into Arroyo Loco just at dusk, and proceeded cautiously, as this was the usual time the boar began their nightly roaming and marauding. A large white pickup, tricked out with toolboxes, racks, and decals on the door, was parked in the driveway of Margaret and Thomas's vacant house, just before the bridge. Had to be the technicians here to render our boar population infertile.

A clump of women was gathered up ahead in front of Lauren's house, and I slowed. Just as I drew even with them, they dissolved into individuals, threw up their hands, and scattered in a disorganized panic. Something was coming up fast from the canyon behind. Helen raced across the road right in front of me, heedless of my car. I set my parking brake and watched her go, then turned back just in time to see my new friend, the female boar, hot on Helen's heels. I started to roll my window down, but the squealing was deafening. Hard to say if Helen or the boar was making more noise. The boar cut off Helen's path to her front porch. They both lurched to the right and disappeared around the corner of the house. Less than a second later, two men in blue jumpsuits thudded across the road in front of my car, in pursuit of Helen and the boar. One carried a rifle-like device and the other was lugging a small toolbox banging against his knees.

I looked around, but everyone else who had been there only a few seconds before had already vanished to safety inside. I was just reaching to disengage the parking brake when Helen came running back, still closely pursued by the boar. The guy with the gun was now on the ground, clutching his shin. Someone must have plowed into him, but I had looked away just long enough to miss who.

Helen yanked frantically on my rear driver's side door, which was locked, not out of an abundance of caution on my part, but only because Shiner and Scout both know how to hit the button to lock the door, and do so on a regular basis. Holding onto the car, Helen raced to the passenger side, and had just succeeded in clambering into the seat when the boar slammed into the driver's side. The tiny sedan tipped, and but
180

for the weight of all of us inside, might have gone completely over.

Both dogs were too horrified to bark. They leapt into the front seat with us as the car righted itself and Helen tugged the door closed. For several chaotic seconds it was all dogs' legs and panic in the front seats.

"Holy cow! I thought they were going to hit me!" Helen yelled.

The boar, just the one, had careened off the car, run behind it, and was heading back toward the canyon beyond Lauren's house. I rolled the window down and checked out the dent on that side of the rental. I was going to have some explaining to do when I returned the car.

"They, Helen? I only saw one boar. Was there a bunch of them?"

"Not them, Estela. Them!" She stabbed a finger in the direction of the guys in the blue jumpsuits, who were at least both up now and walking. "I thought they were going to shoot me with that infertility drug!"

Hmm. Well, that was an interesting development. I had no idea why Helen might be concerned about her fertility.

"Are you thinking about having babies, Helen?"

I'm not sure I even want to try to describe the expression of annoyance and disdain Helen gave me.

"No, Estela. I'm not thinking about having babies. Besides, my eggs are way past their 'sell-by' date. I just don't want to get shot with a bunch of drugs."

She had a point, I had to admit.

The boar hunters came to stand by the window, and explained that they had successfully administered their drugs and tagged ten female boar, including two juveniles. However, there were at least two other females roaming our canyon, and after today, the remainder of the boar were likely to be too wary to allow themselves to be hunted down and tranquilized. That was the problem with trying hunt something as intelligent as boar. If we continued to have a problem, the company would come back out and try again. No guarantee of success.

I backed up and pulled into Helen's driveway so she'd only have a few feet to dash to her porch.

"There's still boar out there," she said. "As far as I'm concerned, two reproducing boar are two too many."

"You know, Helen, there are not really too many boar. They were here a long time before we settled here. The real problem is, there are too many humans, with all of our houses and lawns and cars."

Probably needless to say, Helen did not share my opinion. I drove home wondering if every species thinks there are too many of all the other competing species.

One might think that after a day like that, I would want to crawl into my recliner and get some serious escapist reading done, but first I needed to check my email. And, wouldn't you know, the first unread email was one from my friendly public library informing me that my book was in danger of being overdue and a fine would ensue if I did not renew or return it by next Tuesday.

The boar population was more restless than usual that night, grunting, and squealing, with bursts of crashing sounds coming from the underbrush. They were probably packing to move out of our suddenly inhospitable canyon.

Shiner tried sleeping in the bathroom, his go-to place when life gets scary, but both dogs ended up on my bed by two in the morning. I know this because I was awake and staring at the clock at that time. Complain about a snoring companion all you want, nothing compares to two dogs on your bed randomly chewing on their paws and licking at odd hours. Plus, once they do finally fall asleep, they snore, too.

At about six, Scout had an attack of what I call "dog Tourette's," where out of nowhere and for no discernible reason, he lets loose with a sharp bark right next to my ear. Good morning.

I turned over and tried to go back to sleep. No such luck. Once I'm awake, no matter the hour, all I can think about is how much my dogs must really need to go outside. The longer I think about that, the guiltier I feel, until I finally have to get up and open their dog door.

I should probably mention here that we saw very little boar activity in the following days. The hunt and administration of the tranquilizers was apparently enough to teach the boar to stay away from Arroyo Loco, although an occasional one will still wander through, usually whenever someone is foolish enough to install green lawn sod in our arid canyon. All things considered, I think I'd rather have wild boar for neighbors than the collection of mobsters that had been occupying the big house the past few weeks.

Curling up on my porch swing with my comfy fleece throw Wednesday morning, I stared absently into space, thoughts of the family living in the big house flitting through my head. Then, as occasionally happens early in the morning, I had a flash of brilliance. Of course, it was a family. Malakov had been hidden in the big house by his mobster friends. What could complete the disguise better than giving Malakov a whole family? The FBI had been looking for a single guy, or possibly a married couple, not a family. Agent Roybal had even said the FBI had backed off at one point when they thought there was a whole family there, thinking that could not be Malakov.

Considering what a slime bag Chip turned out to be, he had probably joined the family as a way to hide out too, along with Sissy. They both joined the couple in completing the picture of the happy suburban family.

Possibly Malakov had faked the birth certificates to keep us headed down the wrong path, believing Chip was their beloved son who they wouldn't dream of hurting. Or maybe they'd been faked for some other reason. According to Randy and DeVon, Chip was producing his own counterfeit identity papers, so maybe Chip was horning in on Malakov's business and had made the certificates himself. And recently, Chip's various schemes had begun to threaten the cheery family picture and possibly expose everyone.

I left a message for Muñoz, anxious to tell him about my exciting insight. He texted back, saying that deputies were picking up Kevin in one car and David in another, and taking them to the county jail facility south of Morro Bay. Could I meet them there?

CHAPTER EIGHTEEN

Two sets of parents were standing next to their expensive automobiles when I got to the parking lot. They were wringing their hands, expressions of horror on their faces. Lucky for me, they apparently thought I was no one more important than secretarial staff, and I was able to slip inside unrecognized.

Kevin was visibly shaken, and more willing to talk than he had been before. He rubbed the red marks on his wrists where the recently removed zip ties had chafed. Muñoz reminded him that he was entitled to an attorney, but Kevin wasn't waiting. The first thing he said, in a thin wail was, "I didn't kill him! I didn't have anything to do with killing him. He was dead when we found him, I swear!" This was followed by the usual and pointless, "You have to believe me."

No, actually, we didn't, I thought, but kept my mouth shut. Why do the bad guys always say we have to believe them? The minute someone says, "believe me," ` that's my first clue they're probably lying.

"You found him dead." Muñoz came right to the point. "And you have no idea how he died?"

Kevin lowered his gaze to the floor, cuing me a lie was coming. "No, I have no idea. I'm telling you he was sleeping when we left the boat. I had nothing to do with it."

Muñoz pulled out his notebook and stubby pencil again, carefully jotting down each point as we took Kevin through the story of that night.

It dawned on me that Kevin was being careful to word his statement to indicate no personal role in Chip's death. Was his wording intended to communicate that, although he personally was not involved in Chip's death, one of the other kids might have been?

"What about David?" I said. "Did he have something to do with it? Or any of the others?"

"I don't know, I'm telling you I don't know." We paused while Kevin engaged in a few racking sobs. Muñoz offered a handful of tissues, which Kevin put to good use. With a final swipe at his nose, he gave us another critical piece of the puzzle. "I saw Ashley switch her can of beer with Chip's beer. You know, when Chip wasn't looking. He was turned away, talking to the girls on the bow."

Switching the cans was hardly a major crime, even if you made the assumption that Chip had already doctored Ashley's beer with a capsule of rohypnol. It only meant Chip would, quite literally, be getting a dose of his own medicine. Kevin dissolved in sobs again, and did not appear willing to tell us anything more. There was a rustling at the door, and a young man in a suit and carrying a briefcase stepped into the interview room. He introduced himself as Kevin's lawyer.

We left them alone in the interview room to confer, and so Kevin could compose himself before being returned to detention.

The four parents waited in the front lobby of the county lock-up, sitting on plastic chairs, arms crossed, not touching the tattered magazines. A failing fluorescent light buzzed overhead and dead flies littered the windowsill. Not where they had expected to spend this morning, I thought.

I was in the lobby hoping to borrow paper and a pencil from the officer on duty. I always think through complicated situations better when I can make a map, and so had decided to take a leaf from Muñoz's book and get my own writing materials. Apparently my status as an official sheriff's consultant did not extend to the issuance of office supplies. Even though be had a dirty mug full of stubby pencils and ink-stained pens on his desk, the officer refused my request.

Kevin's mother made eye contact as I turned to head back to the interview rooms, and she stood.

"You're with Muñoz, aren't you? I remember you were out at the house with him the other day."

"Yes, ma'am. I'm only a consultant," I said indicating that I was essentially a nobody, a fact which had just been made clear by the officer's refusal to lend me so much as a pencil.

"I only wanted to tell someone .... It seems like someone should know." She glanced at the other parents, and went on. "I got a call from Ashley Brisbane's mother, oh, a half hour or so before we left the house." She turned to the others to confirm the timing of the call. "Anyway, Mrs. Brisbane is just frantic. She says Ashley ran away this morning, right after she got a call from her friend, Madison. It's a small town, you know? Everyone could see Kevin and David get arrested and hauled off in the back of those SUVs."

"Ashley ran away?"

"Mrs. Brisbane said Ashley threw a suitcase in her car and took off. She's only seventeen, so the bank called when Ashley stopped there and tried to close her account, and now she's not answering her phone. Mrs. Brisbane is just frantic. The sheriff's office won't take a report, and won't go looking for Ashley.

She's only been gone a few hours, but we all know she's run away. Can you make them look for her? It'll be easier to find her before she gets too far away, right?"

"Let me look into it. I'll get back to you." I stood in a semi-quiet corner of the hall and thought through this new development. Chip had doped Ashley's beer. Ashley either saw him do it, or knew that would happen based on what had happened on previous occasions to her friends. When Chip wasn't looking, Ashley switched her beer for Chip's uncontaminated one. An innocent act, even a funny one under some circumstances. Later, Chip is found dead. Law enforcement gets close, picking up and detaining two of the other kids who were present that night. This morning, Ashley runs away. This was not your average teenager-runs away scenario. Ashley's disappearance had something to do with our case.

I found Muñoz in the break room and explained the situation. He went off to get more details, maybe start the search for Ashley. My priorities being what they were, I asked if he could find me paper and a pencil while he was out there.

A harried-looking woman in an ill-fitting tweed business suit, the skirt twisted slightly to the side, bustled into the interview room just ahead of us as we returned.

"David's lawyer," Muñoz informed me. "Let's give them a minute."

As I suspected might be the case, David turned out to be the key that unlocked most of the puzzle. Muñoz slid a pad of blank paper and a pen in front of me, then sat back and let me do most of the questioning. The lawyer explained that David wished to waive his right to remain silent. She was advising against his saying anything, and would insist he stop talking if he said anything potentially incriminating. David's lips grew tighter and his face angrier as she spoke.

"No," he said. "I want to tell what happened. The truth, all of it."

I asked my first question, and the story came tumbling out, not because I am a better questioner. It was probably like that pickle jar that's hard to open until I hand it to someone else, and they open it with ease. I'd already gotten it started. David had probably already been terrified by everything preceding our session, and he was ready to talk.

Choking back sobs, he first admitted that he put the contents of the capsule Chip had given him into Chip's beer that night on the boat. David had no idea what was in the capsule. He only knew Chip wanted him to empty it into a beer and give it to one of the girls. Instead, David emptied the white powder into Chip's beer, figuring whatever it was, Chip deserved it.

David was unclear on the timeline, but after some time had passed, Chip became first dizzy, then groggy and could not walk, or speak clearly. At the time, David could not understand why that one dose had put Chip into such a stupor, but he was convinced it was his fault. His lawyer scowled as she took notes, but nothing David had said so far implicated him in Chip's later death.

Muñoz picked up the thread, filling in with the parts we already knew, and saving us the chore of listening to more I don't knows and I don't remembers. "We already know all five of you kids were in that dinghy. You took the dinghy off the cabin-cruiser and used it to get home to Cayucos. You and Kevin dropped everyone else off and went back to check on Chip. Is that all correct?"

David glanced at his lawyer, but she only waited for his reply.

"Yes." He paused, possibly hoping that would be enough.

"Then what?" the detective said. "Was Chip there when you got back?"

"Yes," David said again. His adam's apple bobbed as he swallowed.

Muñoz shifted and sent the lawyer a frustrated glare. "Was Chip still sleeping when you and Kevin got there, or what?"

David swallowed again. In a whisper, he said, "He was dead." As quietly as they were spoken, the words filled the room.

"He was dead," Muñoz repeated. "When you returned, Chip was dead. And, at the time, you thought he died as a result of the drugs in the capsule you emptied into his beer?"

"Yes, but then I told Kevin about what I did and he told me about Ashley switching the cans and then we knew Chip got twice as much and so we knew Ashley and I killed him even if we didn't mean to, and ... and ... " David ran out of air at that point.

The lawyer began shifting papers around as though to end the interview. Muñoz asked her to hold on.

"David, I want to put your mind at rest on one point. Our medical examiner has assured us the rohypnol, even two capsules, was not enough to kill Chip."

Everyone took a few breaths, but the detective was not finished. "How did you know Chip was dead, David? When you got back and saw him lying there, how did you know he was dead?"

A look of confusion flashed across David's face. "Someone put a sheet over him," he said. "It was already over him when we got back."

"Did you put that sheet over him, David?" Muñoz asked in a gentle tone. "Where did the sheet come from?"

"It was there! I swear, it was already there when we got back! Where would I get a sheet?"

"In the cabin, David. You got a pillow out of the cabin and smothered Chip while he was sleeping and you covered him with the sheet." The gentle tone was gone, replaced by a hard edge.

"No! We couldn't even get in the cabin. It was locked. Even Chip didn't have the key. I'm telling you, he was dead and someone put a sheet over him. Kevin felt his neck, you know, for a pulse, and he said Chip was dead."

Time for the good cop to step in. "Okay, David, I believe you," I said, ignoring Muñoz's glare. "So then what happened? I mean, you thought you had killed Chip, so then what did you do?"

"I guess we panicked," he said. "We tried to think how to hide his body. We didn't want any of us to get into trouble. We put him in the dinghy and we tucked the sheet around, so no one would see it when we passed, you know, the lights and the wharf in Morro Bay. And then, when we got around the point we thought we should weigh the body down somehow, so we got a big rock off the shore where all that rock is, along the shore there? And we tied it on him. We didn't want him to float."

"Uh, huh," I said, as though that all seemed reasonable enough. "And then?"

"We went up north and out as far as we could. We weren't sure how much gas there was, you know?"

"And you pushed him over?"

"Yeah. He went right down. We thought no one would ever find him. We thought it was over. Then we were worried we might not have enough gas to get back to the marina, and anyway, how would we get home from there? So, we took the dinghy on shore and hid it in that cove. We used to play in there when we were kids.

"We were hoping no one would see it was missing. Then we saw the notice on the paper's web site. We knew our stuff, you know, like hair and stuff would be all over the dinghy. We talked about it. Just seemed like it would be better to report it than be found out. We were going to say we found it in the cove and took it out for fun, then hid it in the cove so we could keep it."

David sighed deeply, staring at the floor. I waited, sensing he had something more to say. He glanced at his lawyer, then looked at Muñoz. "Am I going to the chair?"

Muñoz pursed his lips. If what David had told us was true, that Chip was alive when they first left the cabin-cruiser, and dead when he and Kevin returned, David was not guilty of murder. On the other hand, how did we know David was telling the truth? Chip could have been alive when Kevin and David returned to the cabin-cruiser, and they could have smothered him.

"Let me ask you something," I said. "Didn't you wonder where the sheet came from, and who put it over Chip? How do you think that happened?"

"At first, I thought he got cold. He was sleeping when we left. I thought he got cold and put it on to keep warm. We were going to wake him up, or take the car keys. When Kevin pulled the sheet off Chip's face, he said Chip was dead. Kevin's dad is a doctor. He knows from dead. I thought Chip got cold, put the sheet on himself, and then died from the drugs. We thought we did it, and the only thing we could think was to hide the body."

David's blotchy face went white. He stared at me, tears poised again on his lower lids. "We didn't know what to do."

Thinking about the report of Ashley having taken off after watching the boys being loaded into the sheriff's SUVs, I said, "What about Ashley, David? Does she think's she killed Chip, too?"

"Don't answer that, David," the lawyer said. She turned to Muñoz and me. "David is willing to tell you what he knows, but he is not going implicate anyone else."

I guess that was the end of that line of questioning because the detective made one of those rolling hand motions that means, let's move on.

"Okay, so you never knew where the sheet came from? Never tried to figure that out?" I said.

Muñoz leaned in and wrote "pillow?" on my paper. Not sure David knew anything about the pillow either. I decided to see if he brought it up on his own. We waited for his answer. He rubbed his forehead.

"I don't know," he whispered. "There are beds inside the cabin. Sheets on the beds in there. But the cabin was locked that night. We didn't have the key. Chip didn't even have a key. We brought the beer on board with us. We never even went in the cabin, none of us. We got the rope in that storage cabinet on the dinghy, you know, by the motor. We tied that around him, and used that to tie the rock on." He took a deep shaking breath and let it out. "Seriously, that's all I know."

The lawyer was done and declared the interview over. She said a bunch of other lawyerly stuff, but I figured that wasn't part of my consulting deal and tuned it out. Anyway, I was still too focused on what we'd learned and how the new information might fit into a possible solution.

Kevin and David were both placed in holding cells. There were too many unanswered questions to justify releasing them, and too little evidence to bring charges. A "be on the lookout" bulletin had been posted for Ashley and her powder blue Mustang. She could answer questions no one else could, and we needed to talk to her.

"We also need to talk to Bob, the waiter, again," I told Muñoz when we were back in the break room.

"Why?"

"Well, now that we know there was a lot more going on that night on the Poddelka than we realized before, we should ask him again about what and who he saw."

The detective shook his head, confused.

"Anyway, it's time to eat. We could get lunch there."

Muñoz's brow cleared, and he had another idea. "Also need to find out if there's camera surveillance at the restaurant. Possibly caught something in the parking lot."

"Good idea. It is time for lunch, right?"

Muñoz scowled, but really, it was almost one o'clock. We needed to go out to the marina anyway, why shouldn't we catch lunch?

CHAPTER NINETEEN

Our trip to the Bayside Marina to grab lunch and question Roberto, the waiter, turned out to be one of those good news/ bad news things. Roberto, or Bob, as he preferred to be called, was not on duty for lunch, so we had to settle for a telephone number. Muñoz would call him later. The good news part was the restaurant did have security cameras. Bad news, the manager was out when we arrived, so there was no way we could see the recorded tapes. Good news, she was expected sometime. They said "soon," but didn't say that with a lot of confidence. Really, the only sensible thing to do was to order fish and chips and wait.

In between golden french fries, I said, "I believe David and Kevin, don't you? I think they're telling the truth."

"About finding Chip dead."

"Yes. Well, the doctor told us even two doses of rophynol wouldn't have been enough to kill him, so even though David thinks he killed Chip by dosing his beer, he's wrong about that. It couldn't have been the kids."

"Unless they smothered him when they got back."

"Yes, unless that." I broke apart a perfectly battered and fried fillet and ate it, fueling my problem-solving brain cells with mostly fat and salt. Solutions frequently pop into my head when I'm quiet and not so much when I'm chatting. I munched for a bit longer in silence.

"But if they did they, they had to bring the sheet and pillow with them," I said, "since the cabin was locked. Didn't Bob tell us when we talked to him before that the cabin was locked?"

Muñoz extracted his notebook and began flipping pages. I went back to eating.

"Nope. Said he got Chip onto the boat and told him to go inside. Never said anything about the cabin being locked or unlocked."

I finished off my last forkful of coleslaw and wiped my fingers. "So here's what happened. Bob left a message on the Odam's answering machine. Someone came out from the house and found Chip passed out on the boat. They unlocked the cabin, got out a pillow, and smothered him. They tossed the sheet over him, probably as a way to hide the body temporarily, in case someone happened to be prowling the pier and climbed up to look into the cabin cruiser. Then the murderer locked up the cabin and went away."

"Why would they leave the body there?"

"Here's an idea. Getting rid of the body is the hardest part, don't you think? If one of the Odams showed up and smothered Chip, or even both of them, how would they get rid of the body?"

He nodded, agreeing and finishing off his chips at the same time.

"They needed help, and who better to help than the mobsters? I mean, you've got a dead body to dispose of, who you gonna call? The professionals, that's who."

"Yeah. Except, in that scenario, both cars would be at the marina. The one Chip drove, and then the one the killer drove. Anyone left at the house wouldn't have a car."

196

"Yes, that's true. So the Odams had to drive all the way home before the mobsters could start the trip down to get rid of the body."

"Leaving the body there that whole time."

"Yes, that would have been almost an hour. So, whoever unlocked the cabin to get out the pillow, there's your murderer. And when Kevin and David got back to the cabin cruiser, Chip's body was lying on the bench dead, the sheet thrown over it, ready to be dumped."

"Yeah. Must have been a surprise for the mobsters when they finally showed up and the body was gone."

"That explains where the car Chip had been driving went, too, why it wasn't still in the marina parking lot. Either the Odams split up and drove both cars home, or the mobsters did."

I was feeling pretty smug. Except for the part where we didn't have any actual evidence admissible in a court of law, clearly either Mr. or Mrs. Odam, or both of them together, were the ones who put the final touch on Chip's murder. Could have just as easily been the mobsters, too, though. Not all of them could be guilty of murder. We needed more evidence.

The other fly in the ointment was that all of them were long gone. There had been no sightings of any of them, or the cars in which they had disappeared.

And I still had concerns. "Whoever it was who killed Chip, Kevin and David did admit to disposing of the body. Does that make them accessories after the fact or something? Will the kids go to jail for some lesser crime?"

"Good question. Accessory to murder is only charged if there is intention to assist the murderer and knowledge that a felony had been committed. The boys weren't assisting anyone else, and seems like, at the time, they honestly thought Chip had died after ingesting the two doses of rohypnol."

"Dumping the body has to be a crime."

"Yeah, failure to properly dispose of a body is a crime. I'd have to look up chapter and verse. We don't get a lot of that. Also, failure to report a death. Sometimes you see that with a bereaved relative."

"Is it a crime to dose another person with rohypnol, even if you don't do anything else?"

"Simple possession is a crime, and it sounds like David knew the likely effect the drug would have when he put it in Chip's beer. A misdemeanor, not a felony. I don't see how Ashley switching the beers can be considered a crime."

"So, bottom line, is David going to be locked up for a long time?"

Muñoz shook his head, "I don't see that happening. Probably community service or something."

That was reassuring. Nothing wrong with anyone contributing a little community service now and then. Just then, the restaurant manager bustled over. Since we were done with lunch, she escorted us to her tiny office, explaining that she had good news and bad news. The good news was, her closed circuit video data was stored for thirty days as required by law. That turned out to be the end of the good news. She went on to say that when she tried to cue up the records for the Thursday night in question, those files were malfunctioning. They'd either been accidentally recorded over, or intentionally erased. She played the section several times, but all we could see was snow.

She switched back to the present on the cameras, and we were able to see three less-than-quality views. Sure enough, one camera covered the back of the restaurant, the dumpsters

198

and a view of the doors to the portable toilets. The second gave us footage from the front entrance and the nearby part of the parking lot. The third camera aimed toward the marina and caught one corner of the walkway connecting the parking lot to the pier. Anyone making their way on foot to the Poddelka a week ago Thursday night would have been briefly captured by that camera as they walked. Unfortunately, the footage from that camera had also been lost, or intentionally destroyed. The way Muñoz's jaw was working, I could tell this was a major loss.

It was close to three by the time we were ready to leave. Muñoz checked with his office and learned the county district attorney was preparing charges against both Kevin and David. They had been transferred to the county juvenile detention facility, and neither would be available for questioning until further notice. Ashley was being pursued as a fugitive, which should bring that powder blue Mustang back more quickly than if she was only a potential run-away.

Here it was, a whole week and a half into my relaxing summer break, and I still had not found more than a few minutes to relax. Muñoz dropped me back at my car, and I headed over to the sheep ranch to collect my dogs. After a quick stop at the natural foods store to stock up on healthy fruits, vegetables, and whole grains, I would have the rest of the afternoon to myself.

I stopped in front of the roadhouse to pick up my mail, pulling in just as the mail truck pulled out. I parked in the ten minute zone that had magically appeared overnight one night after the new curbs and sidewalks were installed. It used to be against the rules to leave your car there while you grabbed your mail, but now, as anyone could clearly see, the curb was painted green, with "10 MIN" stenciled in white. I regularly took advantage of that zone, even though no one had any idea how it had come to be there or who might have painted that.

Nina called over from her porch as I stood chucking everything from my mailbox into the recycling bin someone had thoughtfully placed on the porch. I moved my car over to her driveway, let myself and my dogs into Nina's fenced yard, and settled on a wicker chair. She was working from home that afternoon, taking an iced tea break, and curious about the goings on at the big house. I had barely gotten started with my update when Lauren and Freda passed by on their way to check their mailboxes. They waved, returned a minute or so later, and joined us on the porch. Lauren clutched an actual piece of mail. It was a check from one of the companies she edits technical journals for, upstairs in her home office.

With a "chirp" of brakes, Helen stopped and parked in front of the house next door. She'd seen us gathering on her way home from her first golf lesson. She clambered out of her small sedan clad in bright red capris—what we used to call pedal pushers—a flowered blouse, and shoes that sounded like snow tires when she walked. I moved to a top step to let her sprawl in the chair. Five of us had collected on Nina's porch, sipping iced tea.

"I'll start my update over again," I said.

"Hold the phone," Helen said. "Don't we have something to eat? I'm famished here."

Flustered, Nina jumped up. Muttering about seeing what she could find, she headed for her kitchen.

"If someone would go to get them, I have three dozen *vanillekipferl* in my freezer," Freda offered.

We sat there for a moment, trying to imagine what sort of a meal could be organized around three dozen powdered cookies.

"Ah, don't we keep ice cream in the freezer in the roadhouse kitchen? Lauren asked. "Or, maybe not any more, huh? I mean, you know, after what happened to Tee."

"We don't even keep a freezer in the kitchen any longer, Lauren, let alone ice cream," Helen informed her.

Nina came to the door holding up a sad half-bag of brown rice.

"I'll tell you what, Nina," I said, "if you have some olive oil and a wok, I'll get my vegetables out of the car and do a stir fry. You can start that rice. Helen, can you give Lauren a ride up and come back with something from your houses and Freda's cookies?"

"Sure, no problem," Helen said, heaving herself out of the chair. "Grant usually eats beer for dinner, anyway. A vegetable stir fry would be a lovely change of pace."

I couldn't tell if Helen was being sarcastic, as I was already dragging groceries from my car. It was a little early for dinner, and I wasn't even that hungry after my big lunch at the marina. All the same, we hadn't had a good talk in a long while. Freda and Nina chopped while I fried and the rice cooker bubbled. In less than an hour we were settled back on the porch passing wasabi sauce and enjoying our impromptu Asian-fusion fare.

I started my update over again, filling everyone in on the latest details. Sunshine sidled up in the middle of my story and helped herself to a *vanillekipferl* or two, silent, but listening. When I was finished, I posed the critical questions. Who did they think had smothered Chip, and why?

"I think the mobsters killed Chip," Helen said, never one to be shy about voicing an opinion. "They listened to the message on the answering machine and saw a golden opportunity to get rid of the annoying kid. They drove to the marina and killed him."

"Ah, what was their motive?" Lauren asked. "Why would they want to kill him?"

"Somebody said he was doing forgeries, didn't they?" Helen said.

"And dealing drugs," Nina added.

"He was risking the whole set-up," Helen said. "Drawing attention to the location of their operation. Didn't you say the FBI knew they were here, 'Stel'? Also, the killer had to be someone who had keys to the cabin on the boat, so they could get out the pillow and the sheet. The mobsters would have had access to those keys."

"So why did they leave the body there?" Nina asked.

Helen shrugged. "Why not? Why bother with dumping it, and risk getting caught doing that? They just took Chip's car home and left the body there. What's all this fuss in murder mysteries about getting rid of the body anyway? Are people supposed to not notice the murder victim is gone or something?"

"Well, I don't think they murdered Chip," Nina said. "They don't have a strong enough motive. And anyway, as you said, they wouldn't want to draw attention to themselves."

"Who do you think did it, Nina?" I asked. Might as well get all the possibilities out there.

"I think it was the fake parents, the Odams, or whatever you call them. They got the message and went out there. They have keys to the cabin, and the car, too. And they left the body there because they'd asked the mobsters to go get it and get rid of it."

"And their motive was?" Helen said, her tone dripping sarcasm.

"To begin with, they are criminals," Nina said. "The kids said Chip was making forgeries. He was horning in on Odam's business. Chip and Sissy were only there to lend credibility to their cover of being a family, and then Chip starts conducting business on his own, so they got rid of him."

"Sissy, too?" Freda asked. "Sissy also is missing. Or did Sissy kill Chip? She also, she could have heard the message on the machine. She could have smothered him."

Lauren had a question. "Ah, but Freda, if Sissy went to the marina and smothered Chip, how did she get the second car back here?"

Thinking hard, Freda screwed her face to the side. "That is a good question, Lauren."

"Because I was thinking possibly Ashley did it, but then I had the same problem," Lauren concluded.

"I thought the boys dropped Ashley off at home in Cayucos," Nina said.

"Ah, yes, but she could have easily gotten in her car and driven back to the marina long before the boys got there in that little boat. She would have had plenty of time to smother Chip and leave."

"But," Helen said, "not only could she not have taken the second car, she also did not have the keys to the cabin. Remember, someone said even Chip didn't have the keys to the cabin, so she couldn't have gotten them out of his pocket.

Freda jumped in again. "Your medical examiner said Chip was smothered with a pillow, right Estela? Little fibers of cotton were found. So how did Ashley get the pillow if she did not have a key to the cabin?"

"She brought a pillow from home?" Lauren said.

Freda shook her head. "No, Lauren, I do not think she would bring her pillow from home. That is too much thinking ahead."

Apparently, no one wanted to argue with that.

"Anywho ... " Freda put her hand on my knee and caught my gaze. "What about this Sissy? Where do you think Sissy has gotten herself to?"

Not sure I should even bring it up, I said, "To tell you the truth, I do wonder why my friend Evan has recently been digging in his yard."

"Ooh, digging in his yard! To bury a body, you mean?"

My response was a one-shouldered shrug.

Nina stared at me with wide eyes. "I thought Evan was your friend?"

"I think what she is saying, Nina," Helen said, in a cool tone, "is that even if you are Estela's friend, she is not above suspecting you of murder."

I gave Helen a look to indicate I might, at that very moment, be suspecting her of committing something evil. She looked away.

"Anyway does anyone want to advocate for these other suspects?" I said. "We have Bob admitting he saw Chip incapacitated. He could have smothered Chip and had a co-worker help him steal the car."

Lauren held up three fingers as though she had a list of points to make. "Ah, do you know for sure Chip was smothered with a pillow from inside the cabin?"

"Lab is testing the bedding now, but they did find cotton fibers inside Chip. I guess they're trying to match those up with the linens from inside the cabin. So, yes, I think that's a safe bet."

Lauren didn't look too happy about that. She lowered the first finger and pointed to the second. "If Bob could have gotten a co-worker to help him steal Chip's car, then anyone could have recruited a second person to steal the car. Even Ashley could have talked one of the other girls into driving back to the marina with her."

"Hey, yeah!" Helen said, getting into the spirit of the discussion. "That's a good point, Lauren, because Ashley had a reasonable motive. Chip was trying to drug her, and then probably take advantage of her. I might be re-thinking my position here."

"One question, then," I said. "The car Chip drove, the one he had at the marina, was one of those two black sedans with the tinted windows we've seen going up and down our hill. We've seen both of those cars up at the house in the days since the murder, so the car Chip was driving definitely made it back here. Also, it had to have left the marina that same night as the murder because there is no overnight parking allowed. So if Ashley and a friend, or Bob and a co-worker, or anyone other than the fake parents or the mobsters took the car Chip was driving, how did they get it back here?"

"Correction, 'Stel'," Helen said. "The car Chip drove might have looked like one of those two black sedans, but that doesn't necessarily mean it was, actually, one of those two." She gave me a know-it-all wink. I had no argument with her words, but that wink was irritating.

She threw me a bone. "What you mean, though, is if the car Chip was driving came back here, how did it get here without stranding the driver. And why would they bring it here, anyway?"

This sounded like a trap to me. Plus, I hate it when people try to tell me what they think I meant to say. I waited, and sure enough, she went on.

"But heck, 'Stel', with that many teenagers, they could have just pushed that car off the edge of the parking lot and into the bay. Has anyone thought to take a gander into the water there? There goes your excuse for why the kids couldn't have killed Chip.

"And I'll tell you what else. You put me on a jury, tell me your defendant has to be innocent only because he appeared not to have access to a cabin where there are pillows and sheets. Well, I'm voting to convict. That's a flimsy defense. There are too many sheets and pillows in the world, is all I'm saying. Those could have come from anywhere."

"I see your point, Helen," Nina said. "Still, that's a lot of shuttling of boats, bodies, and cars, not to mention pillows. I'm sticking with the simple solution. Mobsters got the message, had the keys, did the deed, and brought the car back."

When Nina put it that way, the logic was undeniable. We all sat in silence for a few moments, pondering.

"Sort of makes you wonder, doesn't it?" Helen said. "I mean, who would you smother if you knew they were too wasted to fight back?"

Nina stared at the floor. "Or, who might take advantage of the opportunity to smother you if they thought they'd probably get away with it?"

Helen shot a look at Nina, no doubt wondering if Nina was referring to anyone in particular.

"Sobering thought," I said. "I hope neither of you is suggesting someone would do that just to see if they could get away with it. They'd have to have something to gain. You know, not just opportunity and means, but a motive."

206

"You ladies are being too negative," Sunshine said, breaking her silence. "All this talk about murder and crime. Let's try to cheer it up at little!"

Helen lowered her brow, glaring at Sunshine. "We are not being negative, Sunshine. We are working out a puzzle. What is negative about that?"

"Uh-oh," Nina muttered, "not those two again." Her chair scrapped the floor as she got up, and she busily began gathering empty plates.

"Oh, my, would you look at the time! I've got to get these dogs home and feed them." And with that, our discussion came to an abrupt end. Sunshine might not have shared my opinion, but as I drove home I thought the speculations and insights had been enlightening.

Dusk had crept through the canyon during our impromptu supper, so that by the time I rolled into my driveway the newly-installed motion detector light flashed on, temporarily blinding me. The dogs and I started up the porch steps. It was not until I reached the second step that I noticed the door to the screened room was ajar.

CHAPTER TWENTY

I rarely lock that screened door, but I'm always careful to make sure it's latched. I take the dogs with me almost every time I leave the house, but on the occasions when they are at home, I don't want them to ever come through a dog door and find the screened door standing ajar. And yet, there it stood, unlatched and standing open about four inches.

Shiner's neck stretched out as he sniffed. No one was on the porch itself, and the door to the kitchen looked closed. I am not the most security conscious homeowner, and sometimes do neglect to lock up when I leave. Had someone entered my house? Were they in there now, waiting to ambush me?

Shiner would not be acting as though he sensed a stranger if the intruder was someone he knew. A low growl started deep in his throat. He has a variety of barks, each communicating a different state. This one communicated fear and threat. I looked again at the closed kitchen door. I could hear that voice in my head screaming, "Don't go in there!"

So I didn't. I may sometimes do stupid things, but usually with a good reason. There was no point in walking into a trap, even if it was my own home. I retraced my steps, called the dogs, and we all hopped back into the car. I slammed the door. For good measure, I hit the locks. Took a deep breath.

My cell phone was in the book bag I usually carry, and I had a signal. Who should I call? I considered the situation. Although it seemed like a personal emergency, being afraid to enter my own home hardly rose to the level of a 911 call. On the other hand, I was reluctant to call a neighbor. I didn't want to be responsible if someone else got hurt.

Almost eight o'clock. Muñoz would be off-duty, unless by some chance he was still at work, interviewing suspects or completing paperwork. If he was here I'd have felt brave enough to open that door myself. Of course, if he was with me, he carries a gun, so that would settle that. The drive here from the sheriff's substation would take him at least a half an hour, even at his usual hare's speed. Did I really want to sit here for half an hour waiting to go into my own kitchen? I was starting to feel silly. So the porch door was ajar? So, what?

Of course there was Shiner's reaction to consider. He could have been cuing off my concern, but he was behaving as though he sensed some danger. Over the years, I've learned to trust my dogs.

I dialed Muñoz's number at the substation. After several rings, the officer on duty picked up. He informed me that Muñoz had left for the day. Would I like to leave a message, or have him ring through to the detective at home? I declined, not wanting to disturb him after hours for what was feeling more and more like a case of over-reacting.

Sat there a while longer. I could call Helen's husband, Grant. Ask him to come up, bring his shotgun, and escort me into my kitchen. Being on a timer, the motion-detector light chose that moment to blink off, leaving me sitting in the dark. As my eyes adjusted, a faint light became visible through the kitchen window. Blue, kind of flickery. The television, of course.

My television was on, and while I may have left the screened door unlatched, I know I did not leave the television on.

What was this reluctance I felt to call 911? Wasn't this exactly the kind of situation for which we pay all those taxes and hire sheriffs and their deputies? Still feeling sort of silly, but more confident that I had an intruder, I dialed 911 and reported my fears, emphasizing that whoever had entered my house was likely still there. Then I sat and waited more.

I do not have a high tolerance for boredom. After another ten minutes of waiting, I emerged quietly from the car. The moment I pushed the car door open, that blasted motion detector light flashed on again, freezing me in place for another few seconds. Really though, what was the point in waiting? Telling the dogs to stay, I tiptoed silently, not easy to do on gravel. Taking the steps slowly, I carefully avoided the squeaky top step. Through the kitchen window I could indeed see the television on, and the back of my recliner, rocking slightly. No other lights were on. Wouldn't a friend, or legitimate visitor have turned on more lights, or possibly even put the kettle on, so to speak?

I crept back to the car, that pesky top step giving a squeak as I went. Not two minutes after I'd settled in, the light in the window went off. Even with the motion detector light blazing in my face, I could see the kitchen door crack open. Someone was standing there, long hair silhouetted in moonlight coming through the windows behind. Dreadlocks, maybe. No one I knew, certainly. The figure raised a hand. Was that a greeting, or someone aiming a gun? From their angle, I was brilliantly illuminated. From my angle, it was like staring into an igniting flashbulb. I might never see properly again.

The figure came forward, pushed open the screened door, and stepped tentatively into the light. There stood Ashley, peering at me. We froze like that in a confusing tableau, a stranger on my steps, and me waiting in the car, still not sure how safe it would be for me to get out.

Ashley solved the issue by coming down the steps and standing alongside my passenger door. She reached for the handle, miming the opening of the door. I gave it some thought, but decided it would be ridiculous to sit there refusing to talk to a sixteen-year old. After all, talking to troubled young people is what I do for a living. I popped the lock. She slid into the passenger seat and turned to face me.

Tear tracks streaked her cheeks, fresh ones being steadily laid down. Words caught in her throat for a moment, then spilled out. "I'm sorry, I'm sorry, I'm sorry. I didn't mean for him to die. I only wanted to pay him back for what he did to ... to Madison, and the other girls, and what he was trying to do to me."

She clutched a single fist in her lap. I tried to give her a tender and sympathetic expression. Not sure how well that came off, given the glare of the spot light. I didn't think she was confessing to smothering Chip with a pillow. Sounded more like she was still convinced that switching beers with Chip had killed him. Possibly she even knew now that David had also dropped a roofie into Chip's beer.

"You switched beer cans with him, you mean? When he wasn't looking, you gave him back the can he'd given you, and you took his?"

Another hiccuping sob. "Yes. I didn't see him put that stuff in my can, but Madison did this ...?" Ashley gave me the finger gesture that means, come here. "She was up on the bow, kind of staying away from Chip, and I leaned up there and she told me she saw him doctor my beer before he gave it to me. I only gave him back what he'd given me. I didn't mean for him to,

211

to , you know ...." She dissolved into sobs again. This didn't seem like the same self-confident Ashley we'd interviewed a few days before.

"Did you see David empty a capsule into the can you gave back to Chip'?"

Ashley looked at her fist, not making eye-contact. A few last tears slid down, and her expression registered fear. "I'm not saying anything about David."

"It's okay, Ashley. We already know David put a roofie in Chip's beer. So Chip got two doses. But you didn't know that at the time."

She hiccuped again. "So David and I, together we killed Chip?"

"Well, technically neither of you killed him. You only gave him back his own drugs, which he would have probably just slept off if someone else hadn't come along later and smothered him. Didn't you and David, or the other kids, didn't you guys talk about what happened that night, you know, after Chip's body washed onto the beach?"

"No." Her head moved back and forth. "I thought I killed him. I didn't want anyone else to know. I didn't tell anyone I'd switched cans." She thought about that for a moment. "Did Madison tell?"

"I have no idea. I do know, David thought he killed Chip, too. And he and Kevin dumped the body, and they didn't want anyone else to know that either."

"They did? They touched his body? But then, who killed him?"

Because there was at least one theory involving a return visit to the Poddelka by Ashley, I decided to keep quiet about the possibilities. Personally, that theory had become highly implausible, now that Ashley was expressing such concern that merely switching beer cans with Chip had been the cause of his death. "We don't know, yet, Ashley. Why did you run away?"

"I don't want to go to jail." The tears started up again, accompanied by small sobs. I dug around in the console, searching for tissues. Usually I carry a supply of slightly grease-stained napkins from my latest stop at the *taqueria*, but this being a rental car, the console was eerily empty and clean. I had to settle for offering verbal comfort.

"The detective only wants to talk to you, sweetie. If all you did was give Chip back the beer he'd dumped drugs into, well, good for you. Chip deserved that, and more."

The gravel crunched beside us, and a sheriff's SUV rolled to a stop. The response to my 911 call. My motion-detector porch light flashed on again as the deputy inside pulled his parking brake.

"Your parents are terrified, Ashley. They reported you missing. You need to go with the deputy, but you're not in trouble. You'll be home in your own bed in an hour, I'm sure."

"What about my car?"

Good question. "Where is your car?"

"I put it over there, behind your fence." She pointed to the side of our newish, six-foot, solid wood, escape-proof fence. Not having driven that far up the road, I'd not seen it tucked in there.

"Your parents can come and get it any time, or they can bring you out here tomorrow. It'll be fine where it is for now."

The deputy climbed out, and peered with curiosity through my passenger window. I gave him a wave, and stepped out to do the introductions.

One thread of this tangled tale safely woven back in, the dogs and I took ourselves inside for a quiet evening. As long as I was snuggled up in my recliner with my laptop, I started looking up home security systems and video cameras. Of course, nothing works if you don't turn it on, and if I could get into the habit of locking doors when I leave, no one, Ashley included, could just waltz in any time they wanted and enjoy their favorite television programming.

One feature of the security camera systems caught my attention. The less expensive systems sent a warning signal to a mobile phone when an intrusion had been detected, and a live feed to the phone. The more expensive systems also sent a recording of the intrusion to an account "on the cloud" where it could be viewed later, and provided to law enforcement.

This caused me to wonder if the security camera footage at the restaurant might also be backed up on the cloud, and if that recording might still be intact. It was too late at night to pursue this line of inquiry, but exciting to think we still might be able to view Chip's murderer walking out the pier on their way to kill him. I sent a two sentence text to Muñoz and took myself to bed, veering by the kitchen door to throw the deadbolt on my way.

Slowly coming to consciousness Thursday morning, I cracked one eye and tried to determine what time it was by the quality of light penetrating my bedroom shades. Most times of the year, I can accurately judge whether it is time to roll over and alert the dogs to my wakeful state, but in June, with the coastal fog blanketing the hillsides around Arroyo Loco, that was impossible. If I shifted enough to get a look at the clock, the dogs would leap from their beds and shake their collars. They'd start that thing where they jump from one foot to the other, making me feel overwhelmed with guilt that they had been stuck in the house all night and really needed to get out to the potty area soon.

My decision was abruptly made for me by the jangling of my landline, which I answered while simultaneously jamming my feet into slippers and trotting with the dogs to open their doors to the backyard. I could hear Muñoz droning in my ear, but failed to understand him between enthusiastic morning greetings from Shiner and Scout, and their excited yelps at being let into the yard. I made the detective start over again.

The long and the short of it was, the computer tech in the sheriff's department thought my idea to try and retrieve the restaurant's camera footage from their cloud account had real possibilities. She'd explained that, although it was technically possible to access that account remotely, it would probably be quicker and easier for us to go to the restaurant and log-in from there. I caught the display on the clock as I listened. It was almost eight-thirty. I'd already slept through my early morning reading hour.

For almost three weeks, since my beloved Subaru burned up in a mysterious firebombing on campus, the dogs and I had been riding around in a less-than satisfactory rental sedan. Every week, Muñoz promised he would go with me on his day off, usually Thursday, to buy a new car. It's not that I can't select the car I want, and I consider myself a reasonably competent negotiator. It's only that buying used cars can be challenging, and I have a probably irrational belief that maybe the dealer won't try to sell me the biggest lemon on the lot if a big, stern-looking guy like Muñoz is with me. When we got to the kicking-tires stage, he could gaze under the hood with the other guys and nod knowledgeably. Maybe ask a question or two about carburetors or torque or the like. Today was supposed to be the day I got my new used car, but this darn murder case kept interfering with our plans. Muñoz agreed to pick me up when I dropped off the rental and we'd go together to meet with the restaurant manager and view the video. After that, we could go get my new used car.

Trying to get in the habit of carrying them, I slipped my new binoculars into the pocket of my windbreaker before latching the screened door and leaving the house. Muñoz and I chatted as we drove. At that point, I was convinced the psuedo-parents were responsible for Chip's death, and for one simple reason. That body left with a sheet thrown over it was what convinced me. The mob guys would have found a way to get rid of a body. Only the Odams would have left it lying there, and gone home to recruit the mobsters for disposal duty. Muñoz was noncommittal, waiting to see the video before coming to any conclusions.

"So, where are they now?" I said, referring to the Odam/Malakov pair. "How will you find them?"

"Not sure. We didn't get the plates on the car they were in that day on the way to identify the body. No reason to. So don't know what to look for. Probably the FBI has that number."

"They could be anywhere by now. I can't imagine how you're going to find them."

"That's really up to the FBI. They've left our jurisdiction, and they're federal fugitives anyway."

"How do you know that? I mean, the part about they've left the jurisdiction?"

"They can always come back, but a hitchhiker found the body of the one mobster, the guy who was driving that day, dumped in a ditch outside Watsonville. Shot in the back, lab report says shot through the car seat."

"Egads! They shot him in the back while he was driving? That doesn't sound like a smart idea."

216

"No. He was probably helping them escape, and at the same time, keeping an eye on them. They drove north. Stopped somewhere. Must have shot him while they were stopped. Then they dumped his body, drove on, and disappeared."

I sat there for a few moments, contemplating the scene Muñoz had sketched. "Do you mean they shot him, pushed him out, one of them got into the same blood-soaked driver's seat, and they drove on?"

The detective wrinkled his nose. His personal fastidious grooming habits appeared to be offended. "Guess so."

"Here's another question. What ever happened with Sissy? Does anyone know what happened to her?"

Muñoz rubbed his chin, pushed out his lips. "She was in the house Wednesday, the day we asked the Odams to identify the body. You said you saw her."

"Yes."

"The one mobster stayed there when the rest of us started for the medical examiner's office."

"Probably he was left there to keep an eye on Sissy."

"And she was gone by Saturday, the day house was shot up and abandoned."

"Yes."

"So you tell me, what happened to Sissy?"

I gave the question some thought. "Well, you know, don't you, that dirt road alongside the big house?

"Yeah."

"It goes all the way out to the coast. I mean, you end up on the Chevron property alongside the highway and just across from the beach where we found Chip's body."

"Really."

"Yes, and once at the highway, Sissy could have caught a ride and be gone anywhere by now."

"She could have gotten in touch with the Odams and rejoined them."

"Yes, and if she slipped out one night and disappeared, that might explain why the baby-sitting mobster got so mad he shot up the house when he discovered she was gone."

"Yeah, possibly. Not sure the FBI wants to keep looking for her. I'll ask."

"Yes, good idea," I said. And, I thought, I'll keep an eye out for any unusual activity among those tomatoes plants in Evan's yard.

CHAPTER TWENTY ONE

We parked three spaces down from Agent Roybal's unmarked sedan, overlooking the marina. Presumably he was still waiting for the Odam's to show up, although he wasn't moving. Probably asleep. Muñoz and I, along with the sheriff department's computer technician, were already waiting on the front patio when the restaurant manager arrived. We followed her inside, where she again led us to the closet that served as her office. The technician entered first and took a seat at the computer, followed by the manager and Muñoz. That pretty much filled up the office. At the last moment, Roberto showed up, and jammed the doorway. I couldn't get in to see anything at all.

They chatted with one another, exchanging passwords and instructions. The clicking of the keyboard filled the quiet spaces.

"Um-huh, here we go," I heard, and Roberto pressed forward, further crowding the doorway. I tapped his shoulder, but he was entranced by whatever he was seeing on the screen and didn't turn.

"Okay, right there? You see? Hang on, I'll back it up."

I thought about jumping up to see over the waiter's shoulder, but of course that was ridiculous. I looked around for a chair to stand on.

"That white thing sliding across the top of the screen, see that?" Muñoz said. "That's got to be the hull of the dinghy as it leaves. Time says ten-forty-five."

"Oh, there you are, see Roberto?" the manager said. "You're going out to pull Chip out of the water, and here you come back. You can't see the cabin-cruiser from our camera angle, only the comings and goings on the gangway."

"Eleven-oh-seven," said Muñoz. "Go ahead and fast forward about a half an hour. That's how long it would have taken to hear Roberto's message and get to the marina from the Odam's house."

More clicking.

"Excuse me?" came from behind me, and another large body pressed past. It was the Agent, Roybal. Tall enough to peer over Roberto's shoulder, he leaned in for a better view. Now I couldn't even try to wedge myself under Roberto's armpit.

"Ah-ha! There it is!" Muñoz raised a fist in the air. Exclamations from the others joined his.

"That's it, then," Muñoz said. "Mystery solved. Look at that second piece. Where they're leaving? Back it up to there. Eleven-fifty-three. See, she's even carrying a pillow."

Agent Roybal reached over Roberto and clapped Muñoz on the back. "Good work, detective. This is just the evidence we need." He inadvertently elbowed me to the wall in his enthusiasm.

"Keep going," Muñoz instructed. A few seconds later he said, "There, see there's the white hull of the dinghy, Kevin and David coming back. Midnight, straight up."

Still jammed in the hall behind three big guys, I couldn't really join in the celebration. Fuming, I took myself outside. The encroaching high tide was flushing numerous shorebirds from their feeding grounds just beyond the marina. They wheeled in the air overhead and hopped among the rocks lining the shore. I pulled out my binoculars and took a few deep breaths, calming myself. I would get my turn to see the video, and Muñoz couldn't really help getting so excited. Even if no one ever found out who this Chip character was, at least the mystery of how he died was solved.

I focused on a seagull standing atop a rock nearby. He, or she, stared back at me. I know there are numerous species of seagull that make the California coast their home, but no matter how many of them I see, I can never tell one species from another. This makes it impossible to add any of them to my list. I shifted my focus.

With the high tide, many small watercraft had appeared on the bay. Kayakers paddled across to the spit of sand forming one boundary, while sailboats took advantage of the brisk wind to zig-zag toward Morro Rock. South, nearer the town of Los Osos, a motorboat steered against the tide, heading this way. Even the boats moored in the marina bobbed gaily as the tide lifted them away from the mud of the lagoon. I walked farther out the spit that marked the entrance to the bay, and scanned again, hoping for a bird, any bird I could add to my list.

That motorboat was making steady progress, two shapes huddled on board. I fussed with the knob, experimenting with focusing on the figures. They were just making the turn into the lagoon, heading for the marina, when I finally brought them into clear view. They saw me at the same moment.

I whipped around, pointing my binoculars at the hillside to my back. A sign there said green herons could be found in the branches of a pine there, so I did my best to impersonate a fascinated birder while waiting for one of the Odam's to shoot me in the back. Neither of them were equipped with binoculars, so maybe they had not recognized me. I chanced a peek over my shoulder.

The figure in the front of the motorboat was still turned my direction, and although I did not have my binoculars focused on her I could have sworn she had a weapon trained on me. The driver had his craft aimed straight toward the cabin-cruiser, getting ready to slide alongside. They were going to climb aboard and take off if I couldn't alert law enforcement in time.

It would not have been prudent to wave excitedly and run back to the restaurant with that gun aimed at my head. By the time I'd strolled sedately along the hillside, glancing up now and then as though still interested in spotting a heron, the engine had caught and fired up on the cabin-cruiser and water at the rear was parting as the large boat puttered backward away from the pier. I had to take my chances and run across the front of the restaurant in full view of those on the boat.

Muñoz and Roybal emerged from the restaurant just as I came around the corner. They were still clapping one another on shoulders and laughing, completely distracted by their success.

"Hey!" I yelled, frantically pointing. The rear of the Poddelka was now digging low into the water and the bow pointed skyward as its driver pushed the throttle to full speed. With a spray of water, the boat cut the corner into the open bay. Agent Roybal sprinted to the end of the spit, but couldn't stop them from there.

Lucky for us, the United States Coast Guard operates a major facility at the mouth of Morro Bay. They were able to stop the Poddelka before it made it to the open ocean. They arrested the former Mr. and Mrs. Odam. Both Detective Muñoz and Agent Roybal were quite appreciative of my role in

222

pointing out the departing cabin-cruiser in time for it to be stopped. I elected not to share that the only reason I had been outside being so observant was because I was angry over being excluded from the video screening.

Muñoz treated me to a celebratory breakfast, which I assumed would not be in lieu of a fat check for my consulting and observational skills. After that we headed off to find a new used car for the dogs and me. I had done a fair amount of exploring on line, and knew the dealership we were headed for had a late model Subaru wagon, six years newer than my previous beater, and in a lovely shade of light gray slate.

The dogs were not wild about that new car fragrance, but I figured they would take care of that problem the next time we made a trip to the beach. I had fun stopping at various neighbors' to show off my shiny new ride. A small crowd gathered around while I was stopped in Lauren's driveway. Inevitably, the conversation shifted to neighborhood gossip.

"Ah, now what is going to happen with that big house?" Lauren said, settling herself on Freda's top step.

Helen gazed down from her wicker throne on the porch above. "That darn house is a bad news magnet. We should have it bulldozed. Give the infertile boar a peaceful place to grow old."

"Ooh, what a good idea!" Freda clapped her hands. "A lovely home for the elderly. They would be so, so quiet, and they would stay out of trouble. That would be very nice for our neighborhood to have pleasant elderly people there."

The rest of us turned to Freda with varying degrees of amazement on our faces. Not that we didn't all love Freda, and the other elderly folks already living in Arroyo Loco. It was only, it had not necessarily been our experience that a person would stay out of trouble or be unrelentingly, or even reliably, pleasant to be around, just because they were elderly.

"I hope you're not suggesting that elderly people don't get into any trouble here?" I said. "I mean, remembering our history?"

"Yes, yes. I was thinking more disabled elderly. Perhaps wheelchair-bound people, the bed-ridden, quiet people?"

"Oh now, there's a good idea!" Helen said. "Let's bulldoze the house and turn the property into a cemetery. We could charge thousands of dollars for only a few square feet. And then maintenance fees in perpetuity! I think we're really onto something here. Who doesn't love a cemetery with a view?"

I shook my head. "Anyway, we already have our share of elderly residents," I said to Freda, while wondering if Helen's idea might possibly have some merit.

Nina had a whole different thought. "We could get an agency to take it over and turn it into a home for destitute children."

"Oh, that's definitely what we need around here." Helen raised her eyebrows and rolled her eyes at the same time. "A few more delinquent teenagers. Not that I don't adore the darlings who are already here."

"I said destitute children, Helen. You know, poor children?"

"I heard you, Nina."

"When you think about it," I concluded, "it is too bad we don't get to say what happens to that property." I kept quiet after that. It is true that I've often been in situations where I thought other people should let me make the decisions. I think I would do a fine job if everyone would just let me be in charge.

The End

Dear Readers

Thank you for reading *The Boy Who Bought It*. I hope you enjoyed it, as well as the first four books in the series, *Fire at Will's, Iced Tea, Missing Mom*, and *Deadly Disguise*, and the free short story, *Back for Seconds?* I appreciate your support!

Please consider posting reviews for these books on your favorite book-related website. If you liked this story, your friends would probably also enjoy hearing about it. I am most grateful for any help you can provide in spreading the word about the Estela Nogales mystery series.

To keep up on the news about Arroyo Loco, learn about upcoming books, and leave me comments and questions, please subscribe to the News at www.cherieoboyle.com I would love to hear from you!

Sincerely,
Cherie O'Boyle

Printed in the United States of America

****

O'Boyle, Cherie
     The Boy Who Bought It/ written by Cherie O'Boyle
     ISBN 978-0-9972028-7-8

Cover by Karen A. Phillips, www.PhillipsCovers.com

DEDICATION and THANK YOU! To all of my friends and would-be friends who suffered through countless declines to invitations and unavailability while I outlined, drafted, wrote, tore my hair out and rewrote this and all of the Estela Nogales mysteries. Your support and encouragement were precious, appreciated, and will not be forgotten. Thank you to all of you!

Thank you also to David Gwilliam for his entertaining and educational YouTube video on how to sheer a sheep and get the wool off in one piece. Not a skill I will ever perfect, but great fun to watch. And thanks to Anita Williams for finding an appropriate name for the Poddelka.

70078602R00139

Made in the USA
San Bernardino, CA
25 February 2018